HELP! THERE'S A
COCKROACH IN MY UNDERPANTS

Andy Griffiths discovered a talent for kidding his parents at an early age. Since then he has tried to kid many other people – including friends, neighbours, teachers and complete strangers – with a variety of lame pranks, poorly executed stunts, pathetic disguises and ridiculous stories.

Terry Denton hates .... So he draws them. He was sitting at his desk trying to write this one when his head fell off. It landed on a skateboard . . .

and rolled down the corridor...

out the front door and on to the street...

into the path of a HUGE TRUCK.

But a little dog rescued my head just in time.

Put me down.

The dog brought

Good Dog.

my Luc

Praise for books by A............................on

'Just hilarious, screwball, ridiculous and very, very funny' *Bookseller*

ANDY GRIFFITHS & TERRY DENTON

HELP!

THERE'S A COCKROACH IN MY UNDERPANTS

AND 9 OTHER JUST KIDDING! STORIES

with illustrations by TERRY DENTON

MACMILLAN CHILDREN'S BOOKS

First published 1997 as *Just Kidding!* in Mammoth by Reed Books Australia
Published 1999 as *Just Kidding!* by Pan Macmillan Australia Pty Ltd
First published in the UK 2001 as *Just Kidding!* by Macmillan Children's Books

This edition published 2011 by Macmillan Children's Books
a division of Macmillan Publishers Limited
20 New Wharf Road, London N1 9RR
Basingstoke and Oxford
Associated companies throughout the world
www.panmacmillan.com

ISBN 978-0-330-53231-0

1 3 5 7 9 8 6 4 2

A CIP catalogue record for this book is available from
the British Library.

Typeset by SX Composing DTP, Rayleigh, Essex
Printed and bound in the UK by CPI Mackays, Chatham ME5 8TD

CONTENTS

GREAT FRESHWATER FISH of the WORLD #47

The Thompson's Gazelle.

... this page
is blank.

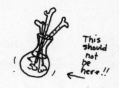
This should not be here!!

PLAYING DEAD

It's 8.15 a.m. and I'm still in bed. I should have got up an hour ago.

But I didn't. You want to know why? Because I'm dead.

Well, not really dead. I'm just pretending I'm dead so I don't have to go to school.

If I can convince Mum and Dad that I'm dead, not only will I have pulled off one of the greatest practical jokes of the century, but I'll get off going to school for the rest of the year. Maybe even for the rest of my life.

I got the idea from my dog. I've been taking Sooty to obedience classes each

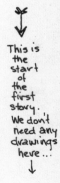
This is the start of the first story. We don't need any drawings here...

...or here.

...or here.

FRESHWATER FISH of the WORLD # 22: The doorhandle.

↓

That's our son. When he died we couldn't bear to part with him. So we had him stuffed & turned into a lamp.

Sunday morning. We've only been going for a few weeks, but already he's learned to sit, beg *and* roll over. Yesterday he learned how to play dead. I thought, if my dog is smart enough to do it, then why not me?

All I've got to do is lie here without breathing or blinking. Well, when I say without blinking, I mean blinking when nobody is looking.

And when I say without breathing, I don't mean not breathing at all – that would be stupid. I mean just taking a tiny little breath every so often – just enough to keep me alive.

The only thing that worries me is, I'm such an excellent practical joker, I might trick myself into thinking I'm really dead. And if that happened, I'd be as good as dead – or as bad as dead – because as far as I can see, there's nothing really good about being dead, except that you don't have to go to school.

Suddenly Mum bustles into the room.

'What? Still in bed? Come on, you'll be late!'

Hello, I'm a pirahna

2

I hear the rattle of the curtains being opened.

The sudden light hurts my eyes, but I remember not to blink.

Any moment now Mum is going to see me. And scream.

She's standing right next to me.

'Pooh, what a stink! When's the last time you cleaned this room? It's an absolute pig-sty! Dirty socks and undies everywhere. Why can't you put them in the washing basket like your sister does? If you're not showered, dressed and out of this house in ten minutes you're going to miss your bus, and I'm not going to drive you.'

She walks out of the room.

I stare at the ceiling. What else would a real corpse do? It's not as if it would make some brilliantly witty comeback, like, 'Lay off me, you old bag. I'm not going to school today because I'm dead. Just leave me alone so I can rot in peace.' Yeah – that would be a good line, but I can't say it because I'm supposed to be dead. So, I just lie here and stare at the ceiling some more.

Next time your parents take you to a fancy expensive restaurant, have an eating race with your brothers/ sisters. If the race is close try stuffing food in your ears, up your nose, down your shirt, in the flower bowl or in your shoes.

JUST KIDDING!

I'm sorry... the editor says that piranha should be spelled PIRANHA. Excuse me!!

Next thing I know, Dad is standing next to the bed.

'Andy?' he says.

I don't answer.

'Are you all right?' says Dad in a slightly deeper voice.

I'm holding my breath. My body is tight.

He puts his hand on my shoulder and shakes me roughly.

'Andy!' he says. 'Andy, I'm warning you . . . if this is another one of your practical jokes, it's not funny! You hear me? Not funny!'

I tense as hard as I can while Dad shakes me. Then he stops and puts his thumb and forefingers around my wrist. He's trying to find my pulse.

Damn! It's the one thing I can't fake. All the same, I try to concentrate on my heart and slow it down.

I read somewhere about these people who use the power of the mind to slow down their heartbeat, so I figure I might as well give it a bash.

I imagine that my heart is as still as a rock. A red rock.

What is the next word in this series?
• FOOT
• LEG
• BACK
• NECK
• . . . .
Ans: Pg 24

APRIL 1ST should be WORLD PRACTICAL JOKING DAY

Try filling your parents' good work shoes/boots with warm custard. When they slip them on, say: "Happy World Practical Joke Day"! They'll love you for it.

4

I guess that makes me a dumb piranha.

A paralysed red rock.

A frozen paralysed red rock.

A frozen paralysed red rock in a deep deep sleep.

It seems like forever, but eventually Dad puts my arm back down on to the bed. Gently.

And he says in a quiet voice: 'Andy – now listen to me. You're cold and you're not breathing. You're staring at the ceiling and I can't find a pulse. You may be dead for all I know. But then your past record leaves me no choice but to wonder if this isn't just another one of your so-called "jokes". If you are just playing a trick, then I'll give you to the count of three to get out of bed and we'll say no more about it. But, if you don't get out of bed, and I find out later that you're not really dead . . . well . . . you'll wish that you had been. Is that clear?'

He's trying to trick me. He wants me to nod. But I'm not going to fall for it. There's only room for one practical joker around here – and it's not Dad. He starts counting.

'One . . .'

I'm not sure I believe that I won't get

DARE YOU
TO STICK
YOUR
TONGUE
IN THE
END OF
AN
ESCALATOR.

so, why am I here?

into trouble if I confess. He sounds pretty serious. I'll probably end up being grounded for a week. And I'll *definitely* end up having to go to school.

'Two . . .'

What have I got to lose? And, anyway, I've come too far to chicken out now.

'Three!'

I don't move a single muscle.

Dad calls Mum into the room.

'Is everything all right?' she asks.

'I'm afraid I've got some bad news,' says Dad. 'I don't know how, or why, but it appears that Andy is no longer living . . . that is to say, he is . . . er . . . dead.'

'Oh no,' she says, and starts to cry. 'Oh no!'

Out of the corner of my eye, I see Dad move to put his arms round her.

While they're distracted, I quickly take a couple of good deep breaths.

'But he was such a good boy!' Mum wails. 'Such a *good* boy! He had his problems . . . but deep down he didn't mean any harm.'

'No,' says Dad, 'I don't believe he did

Next time your friend is bragging, bet him he can't remove the cheeze from a mousetrap with his nose. (Show him photos (faked) of you doing it)

Keep Hospital number close by.

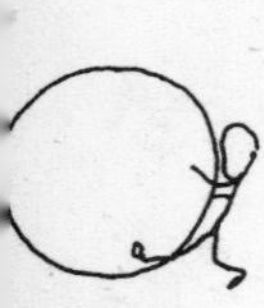

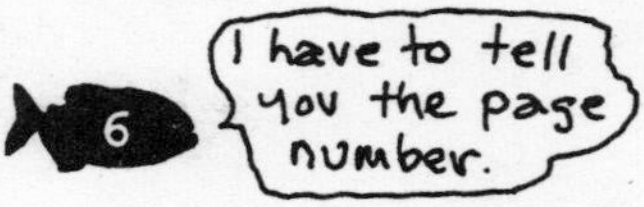
I have to tell you the page number.

mean any harm — it's just he never knew when to stop.'

Dad's taking the whole thing better than I expected. I mean, he's usually pretty calm and all, but I would have thought, maybe, he might be a bit more upset. After all, I am his son.

'Oh well,' he says. 'No use standing around here all day. There's work to be done.'

'But surely you're not going to work now!' says Mum.

'Well,' says Dad, 'somebody's got to dig the hole.'

'What hole?'

'We can't just leave his body here.'

'I suppose not,' says Mum. 'Where are you going to dig it?'

Dad hands her his handkerchief.

'I think underneath the lemon tree might be nice — and it'd be good for the lemons.'

'Yes,' says Mum, 'it's been struggling a bit lately.'

'I'll go get the spade and start digging. I'd like to have him in the ground before lunchtime. Before he starts to smell.'

'Okay,' says Mum, wiping her eyes. 'And

while you're doing that, I'll put the kettle on. I think we could both use a good strong cup of tea.'

I can't believe what I'm hearing. Have my parents completely lost their senses? Are they seriously thinking of burying me in the backyard? Aren't there laws against that sort of thing?

Dad leaves the room.

Mum kneels down beside the bed and kisses me on the cheek. She passes her hand over my eyelids, just like they do in the movies. I'm so touched, I almost forget to close them – but I remember just in time.

'I don't care what anyone says,' she whispers, 'you *were* a good boy.'

Mum leaves the room.

I don't dare open my eyes again. I wouldn't want her to come back and catch me with them open. That would really freak her out. And I think she's been freaked out enough for one day.

Maybe I should confess.

But how do I confess without freaking her out even more? After all, if she thinks I'm

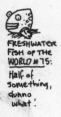

THINGS TO DO:

Why not try to convince your brother that barbells make great floaties.

FRESHWATER FISH OF THE WORLD # 15: Half of something, dunno what!

dead, and then I walk into the kitchen, what do I say? Somehow, I don't think 'Hi, Mum, I'm not really dead, I was just kidding!' would go down all that well.

FRESHWATER FISH of the WORLD #756:

The other half.

But if I don't confess, I'm going to be buried in a cold muddy hole in my own backyard.

I'll have worms gnawing at my eyeballs for the rest of eternity. That's a pretty high price to pay for a practical joke. Even one as brilliant as this.

The lemon tree is right outside my window. I can hear Dad digging. And whistling.

Whistling?

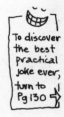

To discover the best practical joke ever, turn to Pg 130 ⇨

I die and he whistles? What is he – some kind of psycho? Normal people don't whistle when their son dies. Then again, normal people don't bury bodies in the backyard.

But as I listen to Dad's whistle, I begin to notice something strange. It's different from his normal one.

It's too loud.

Too cheerful.

And now it becomes clear.

My parents don't think I'm dead – they just want me to think that they *think* I'm

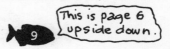

This is page 6 upside down.

dead. All this crap about being good for the lemons . . . that's not what it's about at all. They're just trying to teach me a lesson.

They want to scare me.

Well, I don't scare easily. And I'm not about to be beaten at my own game by a couple of amateurs.

Is your family COMPUTER KEYBOARD malfunctioning.

HOW TO FIX IT.

1. Fill the bath with mud.

2. Screw off all bits that will screw off.

3. Carefully chuck the keyboard and bits into the bath.

4. Stir with a tennis racket.

5. Glue all the bits together again with Hobby Glue.

It should now work perfectly.

After a long morning of staring at the ceiling, I'm pretty bored.

At last I hear Dad stop digging.

Mum and Dad come into my room. I know what's coming next.

I suck my breath in and try to remain absolutely still. Dad grabs me underneath my arms. Mum lifts me up by the legs. I try to make my head flop around in a convincing corpse-like fashion. They carry me out to the backyard and lay me down underneath the lemon tree.

Dad gets down into the hole – which, I can see through my slitted eyes, is deeper than I expected – puts his hands back underneath

 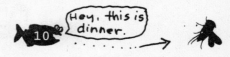

my arms and pulls me down towards him.

My legs follow with a thud.

The mud at the bottom of the hole is cold and wet and almost immediately my pyjamas are soaked through. I'm sure Dad is just dying for me to crack and open my eyes so he can say, 'Just kidding!'

But I'm not going to give him the pleasure. Not now . . . not ever.

Dad climbs out of the hole, Mum begins reading from a small blue book, her voice low and serious.

'. . . Ashes to ashes . . . Dust to dust . . .'

Dad is standing to attention, shovel by his side.

I'm starting to wonder if this is such a good idea after all. Dad starts filling in the hole. I don't have to wonder any more – I know.

First I feel dirt hitting my toes. Then my legs. And then my stomach. A big clump lands on my chest and I feel dirt splatter on to my face and mouth.

Something's wrong. It's not possible that I'm such a brilliant actor that my parents really think I'm dead . . . is it?

A great thing to do in your holidays (especially if you're bored) is to cram yourself in the bowl of your washing machine, preset the cold cycle, & go to sleep.

Very tasty mosquito!!

11

No, that's stupid . . . they'll crack . . . any minute now.

Another handful of dirt splashes across my face.

And another.

And now I don't know what to think . . . because I'm almost completely buried and I'm having trouble breathing.

I open my mouth to shout, 'Okay, you win! I was just kidding!'

But a big clump of earth lands in my mouth and I can't get the words out.

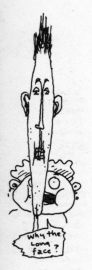

Why the long face?

Hey you, MOUSE! Pull this handle.

It's dark.

It's quiet.

It's cold.

It's boring.

How long have I been here?

Am I dead?

If I am dead, then how come I'm still thinking?

I know one thing for sure. If I ever get out of this — and it's beginning to look like there's

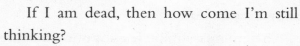

I think the black thing just fell off the end of my nose.

12

not much hope of that – I'm never going to play another practical joke for as long as I live.

Hang on, I can feel something on my stomach. Urgent jabbing and scratching. The weight of the dirt on my belly is lifting. When the scratching starts on my chest, I realise what it is.

Sooty has come to save me! He's the only one who realises I'm not dead! He must be able to smell me, to sense my warmth.

And, as the weight of the dirt lifts, I decide I don't care about playing dead any more. Anything would be better than this. Even school.

I sit up and scream: 'I confess! You win! I was just kidding!'

I wipe the mud out of my eyes and see my parents staring down at me.

They are shocked.

The sight of me rising from the dead has them goggling at me in horror, their mouths frozen open.

Mum starts screaming. Dad is trying to ward me off with his spade, holding it crucifix-style in front of him, as if I'm

Before Breakfast Mechanical YOBA Exercise.

☆ Take your little brother's walkman or game boy.

☆ Pull it apart with screwdrivers, hammers & forklift trucks.

☆ Put all the bits in a crisp, new paper bag.

☆ Say: "Here, I fixed this for you."

☆ RUN !!

some sort of vampire.

'Dad, it's okay!' I reassure him. 'I was playing a dumb joke and I'm sorry.'

But I might just as well be speaking another language.

My words don't seem to be having any impact on him whatsoever. He's still brandishing the spade as he and Mum back slowly away from the hole.

This joke is completely out of control. The only one who's glad to see me is Sooty. He's standing at the top of the hole trying to lick my face. I push him away but he keeps coming back for more, like it's a game. At least somebody round here is acting normal.

Then, all of a sudden, Dad drops the spade and clutches at his chest with his right hand. He drops to his knees, his mouth still wide open, then falls forward on to his face.

I leap out of the hole and rush to his side. I roll him over and check to see if he's breathing.

Nothing.

I place my hands on his chest and push with all my weight, just like they showed us

NO MORE
HEART
ACHES!

NEW
IMPROVED
MECHO-
HEART

SIMPLY SCREWS
INTO CHEST
& PLUG
INTO
LIVER.
IT REALLY
WORKS!

in first aid. I push three more times. Then I pinch his nose and pull his head back. I'm about to start mouth-to-mouth resuscitation when Mum screams.

'Get away from him, you . . . you . . . *zombie*!'

'I'm not a zombie!' I tell her, 'I'm not dead – I was just kidding!'

'Don't touch him, you bloodsucking freak!'

'Mum, I haven't got time to argue! I've got to do this. It's Dad's only hope.'

I take a deep breath. Mum starts laughing. Poor Mum. The stress has affected her brain. And it's all my fault. But I can't help her until I've saved Dad. First things first.

I take another breath and am about to put my mouth over Dad's when he starts spluttering. First a sputter. Then a wheeze. And then a deep rocking laugh.

Dad opens his eyes. They are wet with tears.

'Would you mind sharing the joke with me?' I ask.

'Sure,' says my father, pulling himself together with great effort. 'We were *just kidding*!'

Page 3942.

15

BEAUTY TIP.

MIX IN SOME GLOW IN THE DARK PAINT WITH YOUR SISTER/BROTHER'S ACNE COVER-UP BEFORE THEIR BIG NIGHT OUT.

(In the disco their zits will glow like stars).

HA

And then they really start to laugh. And laugh. And laugh.

They're bent over double like a couple of maniacs. Even Sooty is rolling around on his back, wheezing and carrying on.

It takes a few moments for the shock to sink in, but then I realise that my parents have won.

I've been sucked in.

Sucked in, chewed up and spat out.

But then, maybe things aren't as bad as they seem.

Never mind that I'm wet and cold.

Never mind that I'm covered in mud.

Never mind that I'm the victim of a heartless practical joke that had me thinking I had killed my father and driven my mother insane.

No, never mind all this.

At least I got the day off school.

TRICK YOUR DAD! Tease his nose hairs & wax them while he is asleep. He'll be so grateful.

↓

Possible shapes/ styles

Sorry, on that last page No I made an error of 3927.

GREAT
COCHROACH
HIDING PLACES
Nº 7:
On a piece
of dental
floss.

HELP! THERE'S A COCKROACH IN MY UNDERPANTS

'You know, there's a world of opportunity out there,' says Mr Bainbridge. 'A world full of opportunities, just waiting for a young man like you. Yes, a world of opportunities!'

'Yes, sir.'

I feel like taking the opportunity to tell him to shut up, but I'm much too polite for that. Besides, Mr Bainbridge is Dad's boss.

I'm under strict instructions tonight to just sit quietly, behave myself and not muck up in any way. The worst thing is, Dad has made me promise not to play any practical jokes.

No squirting flowers. No exploding cans of

peanuts. No rubber vomit.

Dad said that if I tried any funny stuff at the dinner table, my pocket-money would be stopped for a month.

I made the promise, but I don't think Dad realises how hard it is for me. See, the thing is, I'm a practical-joke-a-holic. I need to play practical jokes like other people need to breathe air and drink water.

I don't really see what's wrong with a few harmless practical jokes anyway. They help to break the ice. It's not like I've got a lot to say to Mr and Mrs Bainbridge.

I mean, how do you talk to people who think Ice T is a drink? Or, that doing your homework is more important than figuring out how to defeat Sektor in Mortal Kombat 3?

And, as if that's not bad enough, what can you talk about with people whose eyes go all glassy when you try to explain these things to them?

What a snore-fest.

'Too many kids these days,' says Mr Bainbridge, 'expect opportunity to come to them. But it doesn't work that way. Oh no.

Don't Pull This ...

18

..thank the sharks that last story finished...

You've got to go out and grab it by the neck. When I was a young man—'

'Dinner is served!' says Mrs Bainbridge, coming into the room with an enormous bowl of salad.

'Thank God!' I blurt out, before I can stop myself.

'I beg your pardon?' says Mr Bainbridge.

'Um, I just meant, um, let us be thankful to God for such a beautiful spread,' I say quickly.

Mum and Dad are glaring at me.

'Oh,' says Mr Bainbridge, 'that's all right then. For a moment there I thought you were taking the Lord's name in vain. That's the other trouble with young people today. They have no—'

'Perhaps you'd like to say grace, Andy?' says Mrs Bainbridge. 'The lasagne is getting cold.'

'Oh, ah, yes,' I say.

The fork!!

It's been so long since I said grace, I can barely remember the words.

Everybody closes their eyes.

For a moment I'm tempted to say, 'Two, four, six, eight – bog in, don't wait!' but then I remember Dad's warning.

So far there have been 17 to's, two toos and one two in this story. Count them!

HA

'For what we are about to receive . . .'

I know I should have my eyes shut too, but somebody's got to keep theirs open to make sure that everyone else's stay closed. And, as I'm the one saying grace, it might as well be me.

But, as I'm trying to think of the next line, I see something in the salad bowl. Something oval. Something dark brown. Something that looks a lot like a dead cockroach.

At least, I think it's dead. It's sort of hard to tell. All I know is, there's a cockroach in the salad, and it probably wasn't put there on purpose. Unless Mr and Mrs Bainbridge eat cockroaches – which seems unlikely. I mean, Mr Bainbridge must get paid more than Dad, and *we* don't have to eat cockroaches.

'May the Lord make us truly thankful . . .'

Truly thankful for a cockroach?

This would be funny if it wasn't so serious.

I can't just put up my hand and say, 'Excuse me, but there's a dead cockroach in the salad.' It would make it look like the Bainbridges have a really dirty kitchen. They'd get really embarrassed because

they'd think that we think that cockroaches fall into their food all the time.

GREAT
COCKROACH
HIDING
PLACES
Nº 12:
Up someone's
nose when
they first
wake up.

But even worse still, Dad might think that I put it there for a joke. And that would mean trouble.

I have to get it out before anybody notices. For everybody's sake.

I grab my spoon to scoop the roach off the salad leaf . . .

'Amen,' says Mr Bainbridge, finishing grace for me as he opens his eyes.

He picks up the salad bowl.

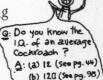

Q: Do you know the I.Q. of an average Cockroach?
A: (a) 12 (See pg. 44)
   (b) 120 (See pg. 98)
   (c) 240 (See pg 122)

'Salad, Andy?'

'Yes please,' I say. Luck is running my way.

Mr Bainbridge passes me the bowl. I scoop a large portion of salad on to my plate, including the top two pieces of lettuce with the dead roach in between.

So far so good.

Mrs Bainbridge places a large slab of lasagne on the other side of my plate. Normally my mouth would be watering, but the cockroach has kind of taken the edge off my appetite.

'Would you care for some potatoes, Andy?'

21

Mrs Bainbridge passes me a bowl full of steaming spuds. I pick out one and pass the bowl to Mr Bainbridge.

Now that the roach is on my plate, all I have to do is get it into my pocket before anybody notices.

But first I have to distract them.

'What a beautiful landscape!' I point to a painting on the wall above Mum's head.

Everybody turns to look.

I lift up the piece of lettuce. But the cockroach has other ideas.

It's not dead.

It jumps off the lettuce leaf on to the table and starts running.

Straight towards me.

The roach reaches the edge of the table and tumbles on to my lap. I try to brush it on to the floor, but it disappears underneath my napkin.

Luckily, the others are still studying the painting. Nobody else has seen the roach's 30-centimetre sprint. I discreetly lift the corner of my napkin to see where the roach has got to, but it's not there. I feel

AMAZING EYE TRICK #2.

Stare at these 3 lines

through a magnifying glass. Which one looks most like the emotion of envy?

Ans Pg 54.

32, 3, 2

a gentle pricking on my stomach. It's underneath my shirt!

I freeze. The roach crawls around my side and on to my back.

I guess I could crush it by throwing myself back hard against the chair. It would probably work, but it might take more than one go to actually kill it and this could give Mr and Mrs Bainbridge the wrong impression. I don't want them thinking I've lost my mind.

'Are you keen on painting, Andy?' asks Mrs Bainbridge.

'I like it,' I say, 'but I'm not very good at it.' I'm trying hard not to panic.

'Ah!' says Mr Bainbridge. 'But practice makes perfect! If a fellow really wants to do something badly enough and he's prepared to apply himself for long enough, then . . .'

'Yes, dear,' says Mrs Bainbridge. 'That's all very well, but perhaps Andy doesn't want to be a painter. What are your favourite subjects, Andy?'

I'm trying hard to concentrate on the conversation, but it's not easy. The roach has

GREAT
C/R
Hideouts
Nº 73:
Inside a
thick-shake
straw

what's
worse than
finding
a cockroach
in your
salad?

23

SORRY, the best practical joke ever is really on Pg 84

relocated itself underneath my left arm. I can hardly breathe. It feels like it's burrowing into my armpit.

'I guess I like English the best. Not too crazy about maths or science.'

'No, no, no!' says Mr Bainbridge. 'You don't want to neglect your maths and science. Keep your options open, that's what I say. Science and technology – that's where the opportunities are.'

Mrs Bainbridge rolls her eyes.

Answer from Pg 4
• FOOT
• LEG
• BACK
• NECK
• DRAJB*

* Ancient Croat word. meaning SMELLY PIT DUG IN THE GROUND

I'd feel sorry for her if I wasn't feeling so sorry for myself. I only have to put up with his bull for one night. She has to live with it.

The roach has finished playing in my armpit and now I can feel it crawling down my chest. I can't stand it any more.

That darn roach could be laying eggs in my belly button for all I know. They're probably incubating in my stomach right now. They'll hatch inside me and burst out of my chest, like the face-hugger in *Alien*. I ask for directions to the toilet and excuse myself from the table.

It's roach-killing time.

flea collar

Well, that was educational.

42, 4, 2. Count them.

24

*

The bathroom is upstairs. I snib the door behind me and yank off my T-shirt. It flies across the room, skims the top of the toilet bowl, and lands in a heap beside it. But the roach is not on my chest.

Or my back.

Uh-oh – not a moment to lose!

I kick my shoes off, and peel off my trousers and jocks in one swift movement.

I'm completely naked – except for my socks – but I still can't find the roach.

There are only two places it can be – one of which is too horrible to even think about.

I study the pile of clothes carefully. The roach emerges from the bottom of my jeans. It's creeping up the left leg. I pick up one of my shoes. Very slowly – so that the roach doesn't notice – and raise it high above my head.

The roach reaches the bottom button of my fly.

I take a deep breath.

But something holds me back. If I smash it right there, I'm going to end up with its pasty white guts splattered all over the

GREAT
C/R
HIDEOUTS
No 81:
On the
tip of a
lipstick.

I bet there's
a bucket
waiting on
the other
side of
this door.

25

front of my jeans.

Not cool.

Might look like I've had an embarrassing accident. I put my shoe down slowly. The roach crawls back inside my jeans.

There's got to be a better way than splattering.

I look around for inspiration.

There's a window above the toilet. It's high and very small, but it might do. I could climb up there, hold the jeans outside the window and shake the cockroach off.

No sweat. No splatter. No roach.

I pick up the jeans, taking care to hold the waist and the trouser legs closed so that the roach can't escape. I shut the lid of the toilet and use it to step up on to the cistern. The window is now level with my head.

I lean against the wall for balance and slide the window open as far as it will go. I push the jeans out of the window and shake them as hard as I can.

Suddenly, the roach is on my hand. I get such a fright, I drop the jeans, lose my footing and crash down into the bath.

I feel like lying here, closing my eyes, and pretending it's all just a bad dream – but I have to find the roach before it disappears again. I get out of the bath and study myself in the mirror.

GREAT C/R HIDEOUTS
Nº 37:
Between the two tallest chips.

The roach is sitting on top of my head.

This time I know exactly what to do. It's not going to be pleasant, but it's the only way. This is one tricky cockroach and I can't afford to take any chances.

No way am I going to fall for that one.

I go back to the toilet and get down on to my knees. I lift the lid and bend lower and lower until my head is right inside the bowl. Then I take a deep breath, reach up and push the flush button.

It's horrible.

Toilet water up my nose.

Toilet water in my ears.

Toilet water in my mouth.

Finally, the flushing stops. I sit back up.

It's gone.

But so are my jeans.

I can't go back to the table without them. What would I say? I can just imagine the conversation:

Blank.

MRS BAINBRIDGE: Where are your pants, Andy?

ME: Oh, I accidentally dropped them out of the bathroom window, Mrs Bainbridge.

MR BAINBRIDGE: Isn't that annoying! It happens to me all the time. Why don't you have a look in my wardrobe and see if there's anything there that fits you?

Yeah, right. Dream on. Meanwhile, back in the real world, I'm naked from the waist down.

There's no choice, really, but to climb out the window and fetch my jeans. I don't fancy a month without pocket-money.

I climb back on top of the cistern and lean across to the tiny window. It's going to be a tight squeeze, but since I haven't eaten any dinner yet, I reckon I'll make it.

I grip the narrow ledge and pull myself up and halfway out.

It's a long way to the ground. I didn't realise I was so high up.

But I'm in no danger of falling.

I'm stuck.

I can't go forward and I can't go back.

And to make matters worse, there's

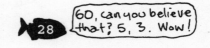

So, can you believe that? 5, 3. Wow!

someone banging on the door.

'It's taken!' I yell.

'Is everything all right?' calls Mum. 'You've been in there an awfully long time!'

'Yes,' I call. 'I'll be out in a second.'

'He's not answering!' says Mum. 'I think there's something wrong!'

She can't hear me because my head is outside the house.

Then I hear Mr Bainbridge's voice.

'Stand back, everyone. I'm going to break the door down.'

Oh great. My hero.

I hear a huge crash.

Mr Bainbridge is no muscle man, but the flimsy lock snaps like it's Arnie Schwarzenegger himself out there.

'Oh my God!' says Mr Bainbridge.

For probably the first time in his life, Mr Bainbridge has taken the Lord's name in vain, but I guess the last thing he expected to see was my bare bum staring at him from his bathroom window.

'Oh my God!' says Mrs Bainbridge.

'Oh my God!' says Mum.

GREAT C/R HIDEOUTS Nº 91: In a stuffed olive (first throw out the red thing).

ARRHH!!

29

'Oh my God!' says Dad.

'I know this seems a little unusual,' I yell, 'but there's a perfectly reasonable and logical explanation! See, while I was saying grace, I saw this cockroach in the salad bowl, only I didn't want to say anything because . . .'

But I might as well be telling it to the man in the moon.

Mum and Dad and the Bainbridges are too busy gabbling on about ladders and fire brigades and irresponsible young idiots who can't even be trusted to sit the right way on a toilet seat.

I close my eyes and wonder if I'll be able to interest anybody in bidding for the TV, newspaper, magazine, film and book rights to my story, and whether the proceeds will make up for the pocket-money I'm about to lose.

One door closes, another opens.

Like Mr Bainbridge says, there's a world of opportunities out there.

DANGEROUS COCKROACH HIDING PLACES.

1.

Between biscuit + cheese.

2. Between eyelid & eye.

3.

On the blades of a food processor.

...this story ends here

...go on to next story

68 'to's, 6 'too's and only a miserly 3 'two's. Wow, statistics can be so interesting.

30

Gorillagram

How to DRAW a GORILLA

I I have long, shiny black hair and big grey feet with black toe-nails. I have enormous hands with big stubby fingers. I have a spiky black mohawk, a big flat nose and a mouth that moves.

Normally, you would find a creature like me in the jungle or in a zoo, but tonight I am loose on Lygon Street.

I am headed for a restaurant called *La Trattoria*, where Jen, my sister, is having her sixteenth birthday party.

If you didn't know I was wearing a gorilla suit you would swear that I was a real gorilla. That is, until I start dancing and

singing 'Happy Birthday'.

Real gorillas don't sing 'Happy Birthday'.

Real gorillas don't sing much at all.

Not the ones I've seen in the zoo, anyway. I guess there's not much to sing about when you're stuck in the same enclosure day after day with all these human beings sticking their noses into your business.

There's not that much to sing about when you're stuck in a gorilla suit, either.

A
GORILLA?
↓

No...
Pete
Bronson
who lives
3 doors down
from me.

It's a pretty weird experience. You feel sort of cut off from the world. It's like you're there but not there at the same time.

And to make things worse, the suit is about ten sizes too big.

I've only had it on for ten minutes and already I'm boiling hot. I can't see properly because the mask keeps falling forward over my eyes. I have to keep pulling it back against my face, which is a pain, because the inside is already slimy with sweat and stinks of rubber.

Gorilla
pretending
to
be an
incinerator.
(Tricked me)

Everybody I pass either stares or waves at me. They're all trying to figure out what a gorilla is doing on Lygon Street. To tell you

 I'm a new fish.

the truth, I'm starting to wonder myself.

At last I come to the restaurant, but I can't open the door. My hands are swimming in these big rubber gorilla gloves.

Luckily, one of the waitresses opens it for me. I feel like I should say thank you, but I can't, because real gorillas don't speak English.

The restaurant is full of people. They all turn to look at me.

Jen's party is on the second floor. I pull my mask back tight across my face for the five thousandth time and hunch over to the spiral staircase in the middle of the room. I pass a woman in a purple dress who says to her friends in a know-it-all voice, 'It's just a gorillagram.'

Talk about a party-pooper.

The staircase is difficult to climb because my feet are so large and the steps are so small. When I get to the top, I look across the restaurant at Jen's table. She's sitting with her back to me.

I creep up behind her and put my paws over her eyes.

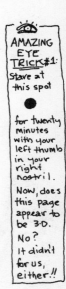

AMAZING EYE TRICK #1:
Stare at this spot ● for twenty minutes with your left thumb in your right nostril.
Now, does this page appear to be 3-D.
No?
It didn't for us, either!!

A very rare steak, indeed.

The other one was so boring. We had him replaced.

33

'Who is it?' she asks.

I don't say anything.

'Come on,' she says, trying to pull my hands away. 'I give up.'

I crouch down, put my head close to hers and take my hands away.

She screams.

A GORILLA?

No, my Grade 3 teacher Sister Scrofulus

I jump up and start dancing around the table. I can't see properly. The inside of the mask is dripping with perspiration.

All I can taste is rubber.

I knock my knee on a corner of the table. It hurts like heck but I don't stop dancing.

I start singing a version of 'Happy Birthday' without words – just grunts.

Everybody is laughing. Jen's friends, Mum and Dad, the people at the surrounding tables – everybody, that is, except Jen.

Mechanical Martini

'I know it's you, Andy,' she says. 'You're an idiot! Go away!'

When I finish singing, I go up and put my arm around her. I growl really loudly and give her a big sloppy kiss on the cheek.

'Get lost!' she says. 'I mean it!'

But I'm just starting to enjoy myself. I put

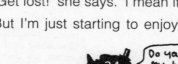

Do you like my hat?

my hand into her plate of spaghetti and pretend to scoop it into my mouth, but I deliberately miss and smear it all over my face. Jen is not impressed.

'Get out of my dinner!' she says. 'I can't eat that now. Why do you have to wreck everything?'

GORILLA trying to impersonate Politician.

She picks up the whole bowl and tips it over my head. Strands of spaghetti and pesto sauce slide down in front of my eyeholes.

But I don't get mad.

I grab a glass of water, drink a big mouthful and, standing on one leg with my arms out to the side – like a fountain – I begin to squirt the water through my teeth. All over Jen. She starts screaming at me.

'Andy – that's enough!'

That's Mum. And she means it.

Time to split.

I put my arms over my head, like I know I've been a very naughty gorilla, and skulk towards the stairs.

I forget that my feet are too big for the steps and end up in a heap at the bottom.

Not a very dignified exit, but a gorillagram

they'll never forget.

I pick myself up off the restaurant floor as if nothing out of the ordinary has happened – as if this is the way gorillas always come down stairs.

Some women are watching me and smiling. One of them is the woman in the purple dress.

A GORILLA?
↓

No, it's the local TRAFFIC OFFICER (Hates skateboards)

Just a gorillagram, eh?

I lope up to their table like I'm the sweetest, meekest gorilla on earth, just coming up to have my head scratched. Then, without warning, I raise my arms and roar as loudly as I can. They all jump back in fright.

It works better than I'd expected.

In fact, they get such a fright that I get a fright myself. With my heart racing, I make it back out on to the street.

You don't want CRAYFISH. No.No. It's not nice this time of year

I was going to go back to the car and change, but I'm too pumped up. This suit has powers I never even dreamed of.

There is a seafood restaurant next door to *La Trattoria*. Everybody is staring at me through the glass. It's weird. I'm feeling less and less like a human being.

KNOCK KNOCK

36

That's better.

This must be what it feels like to be one of the gorillas at the zoo – being stared at all day long. People watching you eat. People watching you go to the toilet. People watching you while you're trying to watch TV.

Except for one important difference – I'm outside on the street, free. The human beings are the ones who are trapped.

I start to imagine that I have just escaped from the zoo, and that I am seeing the street and its inhabitants for the first time – as if the human world is the zoo and I am the visitor.

New Gorilla head bowling balls.

I move up to the window and press my face against it.

I start staring back at the humans – pointing and poking my finger against the glass.

Who ordered SEA FOOD??

The humans are not quite sure how to take this. Some smile. Others just stare back blankly. They're not used to being watched.

An old man and lady are sitting at the table nearest the window. They are not taking any notice of me. I ignore the other patrons and study the old couple intently.

what smells?

They just keep eating and talking, as if I'm not there.

I break off a couple of twigs from a tree on the edge of the footpath and hold one in each hand.

As the old man cuts his food with his knife, I cut an imaginary plate of food with my twig. As he puts the food into his mouth with his fork, I put the imaginary food into my mouth with my other twig.

A GORILLA?
↓

No.. close though. It's our school principal.

The man looks at up. He says something to the old lady. She looks at me and waves her hand dismissively.

I ask myself what a real gorilla would do in this situation and the answer comes to me.

I turn around, bend over and moon at them. I hoot loudly and run down the street to the next restaurant.

I can't stop laughing.

That old couple will probably spend the rest of their lives wondering why on earth they were mooned at by a gorilla.

This is better fun than gorillagrams. I am a gorilla with a get-out-of-zoo-free card and I'm not going to waste a second.

KNOCK KNOCK

It's like dog poo.

At the next restaurant I don't press my face against the glass. I don't imitate anybody. I just stand gawking.

After a few minutes, one of the waiters comes out. He seems a little nervous.

'Um, er, ah . . .' he says in a shaky voice. 'Can I help you?'

I cock my head to the side, as if I don't understand.

'Can I help you?' he asks again after a long pause.

I step towards him.

He steps back.

I grunt.

'I'm sorry, sir, but I really must ask you to move away from the window or I will have to call the police.'

I grunt again and step closer to the little man. He stands his ground.

I reach out and give him a big hug.

But he doesn't freak out. He hugs me back. The people inside the restaurant applaud.

I grunt, release the waiter and pat him on the head. Then I give a low bow, turn around and walk on down the street.

I'm having such fun visiting all the restaurants along Lygon Street, that I lose track of the time.

I'm not sure how much later it is when I return to the seafood restaurant. The old man and lady are gone, but a couple of girls are sitting at their table.

I put my hands up behind my head, start swivelling my hips and singing, 'I'm too sexy for my gorilla suit'.

I'm dancing pretty well I think – for a gorilla – but the girls are not interested. They are looking at something behind me.

That's when I notice the flashing blue light reflecting off the restaurant window.

I turn around. There are two police officers – a man and a woman – crouched beside a police car.

Uh-oh.

The man is talking into the handpiece of his radio. The woman is holding a gun. The gun is pointed at me.

Time to become human again.

'Don't shoot!' I yell. 'I'm not a real gorilla! It's just a suit!'

A GORILLA?

No, wrong again!! It's Peter Lik's reflection

KNOCK KNOCK

40

That's better.

The policewoman brings her left hand up to her gun so that now she is holding it with both hands.

'Stay there, big fella!' she says. 'Don't move. Everything will be all right.'

'No, you don't understand,' I say. 'You're making a terrible mistake!'

But either she's not listening, or my voice is muffled by the mask, because she keeps that gun pointed right at my chest.

New all electric Gorilla. (very handy)

I realise that the quickest way to convince her that I'm not a gorilla would be to take my mask off.

I grab the hair on top of my mask and pull. But it won't come off.

I can't undo the eyelets that attach the back of the head to the suit because my hands are inside the big rubber gloves. And I can't get the gloves off because I need the use of my fingers to undo the press-studs on the cuff.

'Come on,' I say. 'I know it looks real, but it's just a suit, okay? Just a dumb gorilla suit.'

Typical Gorilla paw prints. (This one's wearing high heels)

'Okay, boy,' says the policeman. 'It's okay. We don't want to hurt you. Just want to get you

Page 41, by the way. And where's my hat?

41

back to the zoo where you belong.'

'I don't belong in the zoo!' I yell. 'I'm a human being! I'm wearing a suit, but I can't get it off!'

The police look at each other. They frown.

'What do you think he's trying to say?' says the policewoman.

A GORILLA?

No, it's a dog, Idiot!!

'I don't know, but he sure seems to be trying to tell us something.'

'Almost human, aren't they?'

'Yeah, it's scary.'

'I am human, you idiots!' I bellow.

Then I have a brainwave. I'll sing 'Happy Birthday'. That will prove beyond a doubt that I'm not a gorilla.

I start singing at the top of my voice.

'Why is it making that horrible noise?' says the policewoman.

Charles DARWIN and his MUM.

'I'm not sure,' says the policeman. 'Sounds like it's in pain.'

I hear applause and laughter coming from the other side of the street. A large crowd has formed. And Jen is amongst them! Thank God!

'Jen!' I call. 'Jen! Help me!'

Thank you, dogbreath!

She doesn't move.

'Jen!'

I jump up and down and point at her.

'That's my sister!' I say to the officers. 'Ask her! She'll tell you I'm not a gorilla!'

But Jen makes no attempt to come across to me. She just stands there scowling, her arms folded.

'Excuse me, miss,' calls the policewoman. 'This might be a silly question, but do you know this gorilla? He seems to know you.'

Jen looks me up and down.

She hasn't forgiven me for the gorillagram. Or for what I did to her spaghetti.

In fact, it was probably Jen who called the police.

I know she'll help me, but it will take some serious suckering-uppering.

'I'm sorry for the gorillagram, Jen,' I call. 'I didn't mean to muck up your party. I'll make it up to you, I promise. Anything you want. I'll give you money – I'll be your slave for a week – I'll give you all my Easter eggs next Easter. You name it, it's yours. Can you just tell these police that it's me? Come on,

43

Jen, please . . . this is serious!'

But my words are drowned out by the roar of a large green truck with ZOO painted on its side. The truck screeches to a stop behind the police car.

A group of zoo-keepers armed with nets and tranquilliser guns pile out of the back.

'Well?' says the policewoman to Jen.

'Now, Jen, now! Tell her!' I call.

Jen shakes her head.

'Are you kidding?' she says. 'I've never seen it before in my life.'

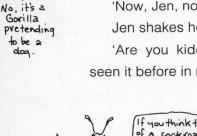

Nick-knockers
Anonymous

Thursday night.

Mum and Dad have gone out and left me at home all by myself.

Normally I would be making prank phone calls, setting up buckets of water over half-opened doors and putting rubber snakes underneath pillows – but not tonight.

Tonight I'm standing on a ladder polishing the light bulbs in the loungeroom with Dad's CD cleaning cloth.

Don't tell me. I know what you're thinking. You're thinking, Andy, if your parents really have gone out and left you all alone, why are you wasting precious practical joke preparation time polishing light bulbs? Why aren't you making prank phone calls, setting up buckets of water over half-opened doors and putting rubber snakes underneath pillows?

Well, the reason is that tonight I've decided to clean up the house as a surprise for Mum and Dad. I'll admit, it might seem a bit unusual to polish light bulbs, but the trick to making a place look really clean is in the details. And believe me, I have to make this place look *really* clean.

See, Mum and Dad have gone up to my school for parent-teacher interviews and I already know that my reports are not going to be that great. Lousy, in fact.

A bucket of 3 week old whale vomit, He He

It's not my fault, though. I've worked really hard this year, but my teachers are all against me. They think that just because I spend a lot of time talking and laughing in class, I'm not concentrating. But what they don't realise is, I can't help talking and laughing in class because I get so excited about schoolwork. I've tried to explain this to them, but they won't listen. It's like I said

New fish. The other one's sick. Must've been something he ate.

– they're all against me.

So what I've decided to do is tidy up the house and make it absolutely clean and spotless – right down to the very last light bulb. That way, when Mum and Dad come home fuming about my lousy reports and launch into their 'it's time we had a little talk' routine, they're suddenly going to be struck by how beautiful the house is looking and they'll forget all about lecturing me.

They'll be so impressed that I cleaned up the house without being asked that, as a reward, they'll let me eat a whole bucket of chocolate ice cream and stay up till midnight watching TV. It's a lucky thing for me that my parents are so gullible; otherwise I might have been in a lot of trouble.

I'm halfway through polishing the second light bulb on the chandelier. There's a knock on the door. It can't be Mum and Dad because they're not due back for at least half an hour.

I climb down the ladder and open the front door. But there's nobody there.

'Hello!' I call. 'Hello?'

AMAZING
EYE
TRICK #3

Stare at
this dot

●

for just
3 secs.
Now close
your eyes.
Turn around.
Open your
eyes.
What do
you see?
ANS: Pg 77.

KNOCK!
KNOCK!

WHO'S
THERE

SPLAT

Page 47

No answer.

That's strange. Whoever it was must be really impatient. I hate that.

I close the door, climb back up the ladder and continue polishing the light bulb.

There's another knock at the door.

'Hang on,' I yell, 'I'll be right there.'

I practically jump off the ladder, and rush to the door.

I open it.

Nobody there.

This is obviously somebody's idea of a joke. And I can guess exactly who that somebody is – Danny Pickett.

Poor Danny. That guy is a compulsive nick-knocker. He can't bear to walk past a house without knocking on the front door and running away. I reckon he should join Nick-knockers Anonymous.

He's probably out in the garden somewhere right now, laughing at me.

'Danny!' I call. 'You might as well come out. I know it's you.'

I peer into the darkness but I can't see him anywhere.

Page 49.

'Okay,' I say. 'Have it your way.'

One last scan of the garden and I close the door. Let him freeze if he wants.

I've hardly put my foot on the first rung of the ladder when he knocks again. But this time I don't answer it.

He knocks again. And again.

I climb to the top of the ladder and start polishing the third light bulb. I concentrate on it to help block out the sound of the knocking.

LADIES who desire access to the best practical joke ever!! Be QUICK! Do not delay. TURN TO Pg 9.

It's actually a very interesting light bulb. An Osram. 60 watts. Clear. A little squiggly thing in the middle. Ouch. It hurts to look at the little squiggly thing for too long.

C'mon puss. Hungry puss. Eat the nice food.

Danny's still knocking, but I'm not going to open the door. It will only encourage him and make me look like an idiot. He can knock until his knuckles are red-raw and he's bleeding to death right on our front doorstep. See if I care.

Yeah, see if I care.

I don't care . . .

Yes I do! I do care!

It's driving me crazy.

Page 52.

49

He knocks on and on and on. He's not going to stop until I open the door.

I jump off the ladder, sprint to the door and open it – all in one fluid movement. I'm going to catch him and kill him. But even before I open the door I know I'm too late.

He's gone. Nobody but the leaves. A flurry of brown autumn leaves blows through the door and on to the carpet – the carpet that I vacuumed only fifteen minutes ago. I slam the door.

This means war. I'll be ready for him next time. Danny's fast on his feet, I'll give him that. But when it comes to brain-power, he's no match for me.

I go to the laundry and grab the yellow plastic bucket. I take it back to the kitchen and fill it to about halfway with white flour. I put the bucket on the table and go into the pantry. I take out a bottle of tomato sauce, a bottle of soy sauce, a jar of blackberry jam, a can of tomato paste, a jar of corn relish, a bottle of vinegar, a can of spaghetti, a jar of peanut butter, a jar of Vegemite, a dozen eggs, a jar of honey, a packet of cornflakes

50

and a small jar of crushed chilli peppers.

I tip all the ingredients into the bucket and start mixing them up with a wooden spoon. It's hard work because the mixture is so heavy and gluggy.

I add heaps of water and spoon the sludge around and around. That's better. And now I have a whole bucketful of the stuff.

I can't wait to see Danny's face when, just as he's about to knock, I whip open the door and throw all this in his face. That ought to cure him of nick-knocking, once and for all.

-Mouth Open...

C'mon Snore! SNORE!!

After about ten minutes of mixing there's still a lot of lumps, so I get out the electric blender and pour a litre or so into the jug. I turn it on high.

Suddenly, there's reddish-black, stink-sauce everywhere. All over me, and all over the kitchen.

I forgot to put the lid on the blender. I hate that.

Once it's all pretty-well mixed, I carry the bucket up the hall to the front door. The bucket's so full and the mixture's so runny

PARTS of the
BODY #241:
The Nose

that, no matter how slowly I walk, it slops over the sides, all the way up the hall. Never mind – plenty of time to clean that up after I've dealt with Danny.

I set the bucket down on the carpet and crouch down to wait.

Danny will be back any minute now. I know Danny. He thinks that if something is funny once, then it will be a thousand times funnier if you do it a thousand more times.

I know how he thinks. He'll figure I've left the door by now. But he's wrong – I'm here, waiting.

SLAM

I'll hear him step on to the porch. I'll hear him open the wire door. And just before he knocks, I'll open the door and give him a bath.

The house is very quiet, except for the sound of the gum trees brushing against the roof.

I've got my ear pressed up against the crack of the front door so I can hear even the tiniest movement on the verandah.

I hope he comes soon. The sludge is making my eyes water. I need to get a peg to put over my nose, but I don't dare leave the front door. Timing is crucial.

Did you notice
my legs??
Cute eh?

A mosquito whines around my head. I grab at it, but I miss and it flies up towards the hall light. I start to get up to have another go at it when I hear a footstep on the verandah. I crouch back down.

More footsteps. He's coming all right.

I move my hand up to the doorknob. I'm so wound up, I'm shaking. I've got to get this exactly right.

I strain to hear him. Another footstep. He must be at the wire door now. It creaks as he opens it.

I can see him in my mind's eye – in slow motion – pulling the door open. Curling the fingers of his left hand into the knocking position. Drawing his hand back. Stifling a giggle with his other hand as he raises his arm, ready to strike.

That's it. Now!

I open the front door and heave the contents of the bucket on to Danny. It's a perfect throw. I've caught him red-handed. He's covered in the stinking gooey brew. I can't even see his face. Revenge!

He gasps and wipes some of the chunky

53

stew out of his eyes.

I realise I've made a terrible mistake.

It's not Danny.

'Mum?' I say.

She gasps again.

This is not good. And to make things worse, Dad appears behind her.

'What's going on?' he says, looking at Mum and then at me.

'Um, er . . .' I say. That's all I can think of. Pretty pathetic really.

The mixture is everywhere. All over the entrance hall, all over the wire door and all over Mum. She's standing there looking like the creature from the black lagoon. The goo slimes off her clothes and collects in a puddle at her feet.

She is just gasping and shaking her head. Nothing in all her years of putting up with my jokes has prepared her for this.

'I think we need to have a little talk,' says Dad softly. He appears calm, but his ears are very red, and they're trembling – that's not a good sign.

Not that I'm worried.

54

Any moment now they're going to notice the inside of the house and see how clean it is. Except for the kitchen, of course. And the sludge on the hall carpet and around the entrance. But that's easily fixed. Once they notice the light bulbs they'll calm down.

Any moment now I'll have them eating out of the palm of my hand. Any moment now. It's just a matter of time.

TELL YA MUM i SAVED YA!

i'm standing right on the edge of this huge boulder, looking over Sealers Cove on one side – where we camped last night – and Refuge Cove on the other. There's a cool breeze. I close my eyes and imagine I'm the last person on earth. It's so peaceful. A three-night bushwalk in Wilsons Promontory can be hard work, but it beats school any day.

Suddenly I feel a large hand clamp down on each of my shoulders. I'm shoved forward. My stomach drops. My life starts to flash before my eyes. Then, just as suddenly, the hands pull me back.

'Tell ya mum I saved ya!'

I turn around. Roseanne O'Reilly is grinning widely.

'You idiot!' I shout. 'What a dumb trick! I could have been killed!'

'It's lucky I was here to save you then,' she says. 'You should be thanking me.'

'Thanks for nothing,' I say.

It's a typical Roseanne joke. Dumb and dangerous. She's been pulling this trick on everybody since we left Tidal River yesterday morning. It's her first time bushwalking. I think she's a bit over-excited. She's new to the school. I don't know why she decided to join the bushwalking club. Probably because no other club would have her.

O'Reilly swaggers back to the trail where the rest of the group are resting against their packs.

'You should have seen Andy's face,' she announces to the party. 'I really had him packing!' Not that anybody cares. They're as sick of Roseanne as I am.

Danny comes over.

'Scroggin?' he says.

OH-MY favorite blood group!

For advice on how to fix a blister on the toe, turn to pg 65

whew... back again... thought I'd got lost.

He hands me a plastic bag full of chocolate buds, sultanas, oats, peanuts and sunflower seeds. I take a big handful and pass the bag back. My hands are still shaking from the fright.

'Don't feel bad,' he says. 'Roseanne punched me in the nose this morning.'

'Really?' I say. 'Why?'

'She asked me if I wanted to smell some cheese. Before I could answer, her fist was right in front of my face, and then POW!'

'She didn't wait for your answer? That's not a practical joke – it's just a punch in the face!'

'Tell me about it,' says Danny. 'She made my nose bleed too.'

'What did you do?'

'Nothing. She's bigger than me.'

'Fair point. But we can't let her walk all over us like this. We've got to get her back. Got to teach her a lesson.'

'Sure,' says Danny through a mouthful of scroggin. 'But how?'

I sit on the boulder and use a twig to prise a pebble out of the tread on my boots. Suddenly the answer is clear.

The author recommends to anyone wishing to get more out of this story, the placing of a plastic bucket over your head, while reading!

WOW!?

BUSH TUCKER

One of my legs has been bitten off!!

Do not turn over or flap over this flap. You will turn into an ugly, pimply, vampire with soggy underpants.

'I know,' I say. 'Rocks!'

'Rocks?' says Danny.

'We'll put rocks in her pack! That'll give her something to laugh about.'

'Great idea,' says Danny, 'but how are you going to get the rocks into her pack without her seeing?'

'I'm not going to put the rocks in her pack,' I say. 'You are.'

'Me?' says Danny. 'What if she catches me?'

'She won't,' I say, 'because I'll divert her.'

There are three rocks – each roughly the size of a small coconut – a few metres down the track. I point them out to Danny.

'Those will do.'

'All of them?' says Danny.

'All of them. And hide them down the bottom of her pack so she doesn't find them until tonight.'

'Hang on,' says Danny. 'Which one is Roseanne's pack?'

'It's a blue MacPac,' I say.

I look around for Roseanne. She's over ear-bashing Derek Watson, the leader of the trip. She has her compass out and is pointing

Urban Bush Tucker

Fresh butts with french flies.

It was my favorite one too... my right leg.

Wow. Vegemite!

Blurp!

This mossie won't eat for months now.

towards the ocean. Derek is shaking his head. Her first bushwalk and already she thinks she knows better than the leader! She is really something else.

Roseanne has this brand-new compass, which she hasn't stopped showing everybody for the whole trip. She's got no idea how to use it, but that doesn't stop her telling everybody else how to use theirs. It gives me an idea.

'Hey, Roseanne,' I say. 'Can you give me some help checking my compass? I'm not sure if it's pointing true north or not.'

She's already on her way over. We go back to the boulder and start comparing compasses, taking sightings on to one of the small, rocky islands out from the coast.

I stall her for about ten minutes and then return to the group. Danny nods and winks.

People are getting ready to move. I sit down and slip my arms through the straps of my pack. It weighs a million tonnes. I packed food for four days, but it feels like I've got enough to last for the next four months. Maybe I shouldn't have brought so much

Although, for you, it's on the left hand side.

canned food.

But I don't mind. No matter how heavy my pack is, Roseanne's must be even heavier.

Not that it seems to be giving her much trouble. She picks it up with one hand, slips her arms through the shoulder straps and strides to the front of the group. She's off down the trail and around the bend before anybody else has even started walking. You'd think Danny had filled her pack with helium balloons.

Even though my legs are feeling like jelly after the morning's climb, I walk quickly to catch up with Roseanne. I want to enjoy the sight of her carrying our rocks. If nothing else, it'll help take my mind off the weight of my own load. No matter how much pain I'm in, she'll be feeling worse.

She's walking so fast that after about fifteen minutes we've left the rest of the group way behind. The track becomes steeper and slightly overgrown. Roseanne pushes her way past a small tree branch that's hanging across the track and holds it back for me.

See! We warned you!!

BUSHWALKING TIP

If you are really sick of walking, try lying down and pretend you've been bitten by a deadly snake. (If someone's got a mobile, you'll get a great helicopter ride).

They want to know what kind of chopper you want.

61

Left FOOT side, I meant to say

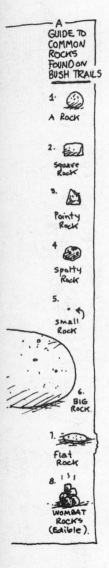

A GUIDE TO COMMON ROCKS FOUND ON BUSH TRAILS

1. A Rock

2. Square Rock

3. Pointy Rock

4. Spotty Rock

5. Small Rock

6. BIG ROCK

7. Flat Rock

8. WOMBAT ROCKS (Edible).

Just as I'm about to grab it, she lets go and the branch flicks back hard against my face. The pain makes my eyes water.

'Watch it,' I say. 'Are you trying to blind me?'

'Sorry about that, mate,' says Roseanne. 'But you should always try to keep at least two metres behind the person in front so that they can't flick branches in your face.'

'I was staying behind, but you deliberately held it back for me.'

'That's cos I'm such a nice person,' she says. 'I thought you'd grab it. Honest!'

'Yeah, right, Roseanne.'

She must think I came down in the last shower. She's staring at me with that stupid grin on her face. And, what's worse, she doesn't look the slightest bit tired. There's not a single drop of sweat on her.

'How are you feeling?' I ask.

'Great!' she says. 'How about you?'

'Fine!' I say. 'Never felt better. You've got such a big pack, though. It looks like it must be heavy.'

'Yeah, it's heavy,' she says. 'But I can handle it. Hey, what's that on your jumper?'

Now, they've both gone !! ARGHHH!!

She points to my chest.

I freeze. Please, God, don't let it be a spider. Anything but a spider. I look down and Roseanne flicks her finger up my chin, my nose and off the top of my head.

'Gotcha!' she cackles, as I jerk backwards – which is not a good move, considering how heavy my pack is. The next thing I know I'm falling off the track and crashing through the scrub.

I'm in a prickle bush. I can't get up. I'm on my back, just like an upside-down tortoise.

'Enjoy your trip?' calls Roseanne.

'Shut ya face,' I say.

'Are you all right?'

'I don't know,' I say. 'I can't get up.'

'Hang on,' she says. She shrugs off her pack and slides down the bank commando-style. 'Give me your hand.'

The thought of having to hold Roseanne's hand is only marginally more appealing than having to hold a live funnel-web spider, but I'm not exactly in a position to refuse.

Her grip is strong and she pulls me up easily. But I can't put any weight on my left foot. I

completely

have to sit straight back down.

'Where does it hurt?' says Roseanne.

'My ankle. I think it's broken.'

'Take your boot off and let's have a look,' she says.

I undo my boot-laces and slip my sock off.

'Yeah, it's pretty swollen,' she says. 'But it's not broken. You're going to need a bandage, though. I've got one in my pack.'

Roseanne climbs back up the bank, grabs her first-aid kit and is back in a flash.

She puts a cream-coloured bandage on the top of my foot and wraps it around twice. Then she winds it around my ankle and back under and over my foot again, in a figure-eight motion.

'Where did you learn to do that?' I ask.

'I'm doing my queen scout training,' she informs me matter-of-factly.

'I didn't know that,' I say.

'You didn't ask.'

At last the others catch up.

'What's going on?' asks Derek, craning his neck to see what we're doing. 'You two playing footsie?'

Help. They've just come out my mouth.

'He's hurt his ankle,' says Roseanne. 'Pretty bad too.'

'Can he walk?' asks Derek.

'Not properly,' she says. 'But he can lean on me. He won't be able to carry his pack, though. We'll have to unpack it and share the load around.'

Lean on her? Is she crazy? I can't believe what I'm hearing.

'It's okay,' I say. 'I'll be all right.'

But Roseanne's not listening.

She's lugged my pack up to the trail and is distributing its contents amongst the other walkers.

'Hey,' she says. 'What are you carrying these for?'

She's holding up three rocks, each the size of a small coconut.

I don't believe it.

I can't believe it.

I won't believe it.

Could Danny be that stupid?

This calls for some quick thinking. I don't want to end up looking like an idiot in front of the whole group.

Trapdoor Spider Hole

Step 1.
Step 2. Rub salt into wound.

Get back where you belong!

65

'I can explain,' I say, trying to act like it's the most normal thing in the world to carry rocks in your pack. 'See, I'm a rock collector and . . .'

But Roseanne is shaking her head.

'Why put the rocks in your pack?' she says. 'Why not carry them in your head with the rest of the collection?'

Everybody starts laughing. Everybody, that is, except me. And Danny. This is all his fault. I should never have trusted him.

If only he had never had the stupid idea of putting rocks in her pack in the first place!

After Roseanne finishes distributing the contents of my pack, she slides back down the bank.

'Put your arm around my neck,' she says. 'I'll help you up.'

My arm? Her neck? She's got to be kidding.

'No, it's okay, thanks,' I say. 'I think I can walk now.'

'Suit yourself,' she says.

I grab a small tree and start to pull myself up the bank. But the pain in my ankle is too

It's growing back.

much. I miss my footing and fall backwards.

Roseanne lifts me up, places my arm over her shoulder and helps me up the bank.

She might be a pain in the bum, but I've got to hand it to her: she knows how to handle an emergency.

Danny is standing at the side of the trail, looking sheepish.

'Maggot-brained moron!' I hiss at him.

He just shrugs. He knows it's the truth.

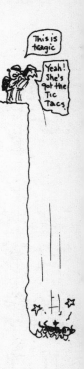

As I limp alongside Roseanne, we talk. She tells me that this is the sixth school she's been to.

'You've got kicked out of five schools?' I ask.

'I wasn't kicked out,' she says. 'We keep moving. Dad's a structural engineer. He has to keep moving to where the work is. We never stay in the one spot for more than a year or two.'

'Isn't that hard?' I ask.

'A bit,' she says. 'It's kind of lonely.'

After a long afternoon we've finally made it

to Waterloo Bay. Roseanne hasn't stopped talking and cracking jokes the whole way. Some of them are almost funny, too.

We're the last ones in. I stagger on to the beach and into the camping area behind the sand dunes.

'There you go,' says Roseanne. 'How's your ankle feeling?'

'A bit better.'

'Reckon you'll be all right for tomorrow?'

'I hope so,' I say.

'Well, if not, give me a yell.'

You know, I hate to admit it but, even with all her stupid practical jokes and wisecracks, Roseanne's not so bad. In fact, to tell the truth, I'm kind of starting to like her.

'Thanks, Roseanne. I owe you one.'

'You don't owe me anything,' she says, putting her hand on my shoulder. 'But could you just do me one small favour?'

'What's that?' I say.

She gives me this big cheesy grin and winks. 'Tell ya mum I saved ya!'

BEACH-
COMBERS
GUIDE TO
SHELLS

1. PiPPi

2. BIGGER PiPPi

3. TWISTED PiPPi

4. LIGHT ALE PiPPi

6. Recycle PiPPi

5. .22 PiPPi

7. WEIRD!!

8. THONG FISH

9. MORE WOMBAT ROCKS

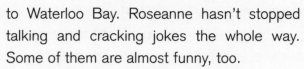

what..?

68

Emergency spew relish

I t's the last week of school holidays and I'm flying to Mildura to visit my grandparents.

I'm on one of those little thirty-six seater planes.

I've got a window seat, but I want the seat next to me as well. I want to spread out and get comfortable.

I don't think anybody's going to sit there now, but I've laid a piece of rubber dog pooh on the seat, just to make sure.

I'm doing really well. It's almost time for take-off and nobody's sat there yet, and there are still two empty seats behind me.

If the plane starts to plummet, do up your seat belt. It won't save your life, but it'll make it easier to find the bodies.

MEN ONLY! The best PRACTICAL JOKE EVER has been moved to keep it from the prying eyes of uninitiated females. GO TO Pg. 9 (nine) NOW!

An old lady boards the plane and shuffles down the aisle.

With a bit of luck, she'll take the seat behind me and then the air hostess will close the door and I can relax.

But the old lady stops right next to me. I can't believe it.

'No! No! No!' I'm thinking. 'Keep going!'

'Excuse me,' she says, 'is this seat taken?'

'Um, er, no, not exactly,' I say, 'but I don't think I'd sit in it if I was you . . . it's not very clean.'

The old lady bends over and pats the seat. She finds the dog pooh, picks it up and strokes it.

'It's only a piece of rubber dog pooh,' she says. 'I suppose it's some young person's idea of a joke.'

She puts the pooh into an air-sickness bag hanging in front of the seat.

Pretty cool old lady. But how did she know it was only rubber? That's the very best quality rubber dog pooh money can buy. That stuff even fools my dog.

'So I can sit here, after all,' she says. 'You

Rubber dogs don't do poo.

70

don't mind, do you?'

I want to say, 'Yes, actually, I do mind! There are plenty of empty seats! Why don't you go and sit in one of them?'

But I don't want to be rude – especially not to an old lady. And I can't just get up and go and sit in one of the empty seats myself, because she might think I'm being nasty. She might be really lonely and not have any friends, and me going to another seat might be the last straw.

It's going to have to be her who moves.

She puts her handbag underneath her seat and settles in with a tin of Kool Mints.

This is going to require some pretty quick thinking.

At last the doors are shut and the air hostess welcomes us on board. She points out the emergency exits and life-jackets and oxygen masks. Some welcome, but it does give me an idea.

The engines start up and fill the plane with their low vibrations.

'I hope it's not too rough a ride,' I say, 'because I'm a hopeless air traveller. I

71

practically get sick even thinking about planes.'

'What?' she says. 'You'll have to speak up!'

I lean close to her old wrinkled ear.

'I said, I'm a hopeless air traveller! I always get sick on planes.'

The old lady smiles.

'That's good then,' she says. 'We can look after each other. I'm not much of a one for air travel either!'

Oh great. Just lovely. Not only does she take up my seat, now she's threatening to get sick all over me as well.

The plane shudders and moves forward with a groan.

Take-off is my favourite part.

The captain's voice comes over the speakers:

'Good morning and thank you for flying with Southern Australia Airlines. We have almost perfect conditions for our flight to Mildura this morning. We'll be cruising at around five thousand metres, at a speed of five hundred kilometres per hour. We have a slight tail wind and we expect to reach our

We just fill up with gas

Now they're turning into wheels!

destination in just under an hour. We hope you have a pleasant flight.'

'What did he say?' says the lady. 'What did he say?'

'He said it's going to be pretty rough,' I tell her. 'Hurricanes and tornadoes are expected. He said to hold tight and just hope and pray that you're not sitting next to someone who's prone to air-sickness. He said that it's okay if you want to change seats when the plane stops climbing in a few minutes.'

'Well, I'm not going to change seats,' says the lady. 'I thank God that I'm sitting next to a big, strong man like you. I'd be too scared to sit by myself in conditions like this.'

The plane finishes its long slow taxi out to the runway. It turns and then starts rushing forward. I can feel my body being drawn back hard against the seat as the wheels leave the tarmac and we climb steeply into the sky.

The pilot is right, of course. It's one of the smoothest take-offs ever. But I jiggle and shake and rattle the seats to make it

seem really wild and rough.

'Ooohhh,' I groan. 'Oooooohhhhh. I feel sick already. Are you sure you don't want to change seats?'

'No, love,' she says, taking my hand in hers. 'I'll look after you.'

Oh no! What did I do to deserve this? Now she wants to be my mum!

This calls for serious evasive action.

Forget the emergency life jackets and the emergency oxygen masks. They are absolutely no use to me.

This situation calls for the emergency corn relish.

Actually, I don't call corn relish 'corn relish'. I call it 'spew relish'. Because, as far as I'm concerned, the only difference between corn relish and spew is that corn relish comes in a jar.

It looks like spew.

It smells like spew.

It even tastes like spew.

The only thing more like spew than corn relish is custard, and I don't even want to think about that because it will

really make me spew.

Anyway, I always carry a jar of spew relish with me for emergencies just like this.

I slide my hand out of the old lady's.

'It's okay now, thank you,' I say. 'I'm feeling much better all of a sudden.'

'Well, you just let me know if there's anything I can do for you,' she says.

The air hostess unbuckles herself from her seat and starts her mad rush to offer us all drinks and food. The flight usually only lasts about an hour. As soon as she's finished giving out teas, coffees, fruit juices, cans of drink and biscuits in cellophane, it'll be time to collect all the left-overs, pack everything up and strap herself back into her seat, ready for touch-down.

She approaches our seat.

The old lady orders a cup of tea and biscuits. I want to order one of everything, but I can't. For the old spew relish trick to work, I've got to convince her that I'm too sick to eat.

'Nothing for me,' I say to the air hostess. 'Maybe just a little water.'

75

what's that trailer doing there?

The hostess returns with the tea. While the old lady's busy adding her sugar and milk, I reach down to my bag and dig out my jar of spew relish.

By the time I'm through, this old lady is not going to want to sit next to me.

She's not going to even want to sit on the same plane as me.

In fact, I'll make sure she never even wants to *go* on a plane again.

I'm bent over, facing the wall of the plane so the old lady can't see what I'm doing. I screw the lid off the jar. I pinch my nose and tip the jar of spew relish up to my mouth. I try to suck in as much as I can without swallowing. I manage to get about half the jar in. Lucky I've got such a big mouth.

I put the lid on the jar and tuck it back into my bag.

I sit back in my seat, hold my belly and moan quietly.

'Are you all right?' says the old lady.

I can't answer, of course, because my mouth's full.

I just groan, louder this time.

'Do you need a sick bag?' she says.

I nod.

She grabs a bag from in front of her – the one with my rubber dog pooh in it – and passes it to me.

I rock back and forth and puff out my cheeks and then pretend to splurk up into the bag. Not that it all goes into the bag, of course.

I take care to dribble some down my chin and on to my T-shirt.

'Oh, you poor thing,' says the old lady. 'You poor old thing.'

Huh? *She's* calling *me* old?

'I'm okay now, thanks,' I say. 'That feels much better.'

'You know, it's funny,' she says, 'but I'm not feeling sick at all. This is one of the smoothest flights I've ever had. You must have a very delicate stomach.'

'Extremely delicate,' I say. 'But I'm really hungry now.'

'Oh, what a pity,' she says. 'You're too late to order any morning tea.'

'That's okay,' I say. 'I brought my own. Could I borrow your teaspoon?'

'Why certainly,' she says. 'Here you are.'

I take the teaspoon. This is it. Any minute now she'll be out of her seat like a rocket.

'Well, down the hatch.'

I open the neck of the sick bag and dip the spoon in. I scoop up a spoonful of spew relish and pull it out of the bag. I pass the spoon under my nose a couple of times and sniff deeply.

'Ahhh!' I say, smiling. 'I love it when it's nice and warm and fresh.'

I open my mouth very slowly. I put the teaspoon on my tongue and close my mouth. Then I slowly draw the teaspoon out and lick it clean, making sure I get every last drop. I close my eyes and sigh, as if I'm in heaven.

I open my eyes. I expect to see the seat next to me empty. I expect the old lady to be as far away from me as possible, and warning everybody else to stay away too.

But the seat is not empty.

The old lady is still there. Still watching.

'Was that nice?' she asks.

'It was beautiful,' I say. 'Tasted even better going down than it did coming up.'

78

'That's nice,' she says. 'I'm glad. Have some more.'

What?

If she'd said, 'Let's take our clothes off and run up and down the aisle,' I would only have been half as surprised.

'Um, okay, thanks. I will.'

I eat another spoonful. Only this time I finish with a big belch.

'Excuse me,' I say.

'Oh, don't mention it,' says the old lady. 'In some countries, it's good manners to burp after a meal. It's considered a compliment to the cook.'

This old lady is unshakeable. If she thinks this is normal, I'd hate to see mealtimes at her house.

This calls for some serious grossering-outering.

I get another spoonful and, instead of putting it in my mouth, I plonk it on top of my head.

'Makes great shampoo, too,' I say. 'Or should I say "sham-spew"?'

The old lady just nods.

79

I load up my spoon again, and this time I splatter spew relish all over my face. I rub it into my eyes, my cheeks, my ears.

'I reckon it's just a great all-round beauty cream,' I say. 'Do you find that gross?'

The old lady just looks on, a slight smile on her face.

'No,' she says calmly. 'In fact, I'd love to try some of this amazing food that doubles as a beauty cream. What do you call it?'

The penny drops.

I hold up three fingers in front of her face.

'How many fingers am I holding up?' I ask her.

She pauses.

'I don't know, dear. I'm blind. Why do you ask?'

'No reason,' I say, trying not to gag from the stench of the spew relish, which I just know I'm not going to be able to get out of my skin and hair for months. 'No reason at all. But I think I'm going to be sick again.'

'Oh, you poor thing,' says the old lady, passing me another sick bag. 'You poor old thing.'

BEAT THE BOMB!

Danny and I are about to play the most wicked joke in history. We've been working on it all morning. We owe the idea to my mum.

Mum listens to the radio non-stop. It's always going in the kitchen. Wouldn't be so bad if she listened to something good, like Triple J, but she prefers the golden-oldie station Triple B. The B stands for Boredom. Talk about sad music. It's so sad and boring they have to run competitions all the time to bribe people to listen to it.

They've got this competition at the moment called Beat the Bomb. Every hour

they ring up a listener and then start the clock ticking. Every few seconds, over the sound of the clock, a voice says ever-increasing amounts of money, like 'One hundred dollars . . . one hundred and fifty-five dollars . . . two hundred and three dollars . . .' and so on. The listener has to tell the DJ when to stop, and if they do it before the bomb explodes, then they get to keep that amount of money. It can last anywhere from a couple of seconds to half a minute.

AMAZING EYE TRICK #1 ANSWER

It's very hard to see (with your eyes closed), but the circle should appear more round.

The trick is having the nerve to let the clock tick for as long as possible. I've never heard anyone win more than a few hundred dollars, but still, that'd buy a lot of CDs, a heap of chocolate, and a lot of drag-racing at Timezone.

All you have to do to be in it is send a letter with your name and telephone number into Triple B. If they draw yours from the barrel they ring you and you get a chance to play.

I've sent in about fifteen envelopes. I reckon that makes me fifteen times more likely to win. I don't think anybody else would

BLAH BLAH BLAH

be clever enough to have thought of that.

But in the meantime – while I wait for them to call – Danny and I are going to have some fun. We've recorded the station signature tune, a couple of advertisements and a couple of songs. And I can do a pretty convincing imitation of a DJ when I try. We're going to ring Marvin Bonwick and pretend that he's about to play Beat the Bomb.

Why Marvin Bonwick? Because we always play jokes on Marvin Bonwick. He takes everything so seriously. We use his name whenever we get the chance. Like writing comments on the service evaluation cards at Kentucky Fried Chicken. We always write dumb things like: This KFC shop stinks. I wanted fish, but the cashier wouldn't give me any. She said you've got nothing but chicken. That sucks! Yours sincerely, Marvin Bonwick. P.S. What does KFC stand for anyway?

We always supply his full name, address and phone number. I'd give anything to hear what they say when they call him up to discuss his comments.

'Let's do it,' says Danny. 'It's ten past four.'

'Okay,' I say. I pick up the receiver and start punching the buttons.

Danny is laughing.

'Hey, shut up,' I say. 'It's ringing!'

'Hello?'

It's a woman speaking. Must be his mother.

'Hello – it's Chris Robbins from Triple B FM,' I say in my radio voice. 'Could I speak to Marvin Bonwick, please?'

'Yes, just a minute.'

'Marvin!' she calls. 'Telephone!'

'He'll be with you in a minute,' she says. 'Marvin!'

Knowing Marvin, he's probably doing homework.

Finally he picks up the phone.

'Hello?'

'Marvin Bonwick?'

'Yes.'

'Chris Robbins from Triple B FM here. How are you doing?'

'Good, mate . . . What did you say your name was?'

...and some grilled flake...

DUE TO UNFORESEEN CIRCUMSTANCES the best practical joke ever is now on:

1. Female version Pg.111.
2. Male Version Pg.125.

'Chris Robbins. Your name's been drawn this hour to play Beat the Bomb.'

'Beat the what?'

'Beat the Bomb!'

'What's that, mate?'

'You know, our competition. You should know – you entered it. I've got an envelope here with your name on it.'

'I don't remember doing that.'

'Well, maybe a friend did it for you. Would you like to have a go?'

'Yeah, mate,' he says. 'No worries, mate.'

'Well, stand by, we're about to go to air. I'll just play a couple of ads and a station ID and then you're on. Oh, and by the way, Marvin?'

'Yes?'

'Turn your radio off. We will be transmitting on a ten-second delay and it can get very confusing.'

I point at Danny. He presses the tape-recorder. It starts into a jingle for Cheapies carpet-cleaning service. I put the phone right next to the speaker.

'I think we've got him!' I whisper to Danny.

This book is printed on paper made from 100% Dolphin Skin (Recycled).

PARTS OF THE BODY #121

The finger. (Really a crocodile pretending)

I'm bored.

The carpet ad finishes and one for a supermarket starts. Then the Triple B station ID comes on. It sounds really spacey – like comets and meteorites whizzing past your ears.

'Triple B – taking you back to the sixties and seventies . . .' says the voice-over. The sound of the meteorites ends in a shower of xylophone notes. It's the only exciting sound on the whole station.

AMAZING
EYE
TRICKS #4:

Stare at
the space
between
these shapes.

Does it
remind
you of
anything?
Ans: Pg 102

'Good afternoon,' I say. 'Chris Robbins with you on Triple B, and to play Beat the Bomb this hour we have Marvin Bonwick on the line. How are you doin', Marvy?'

'Good, mate.'

'Great! What are you up to this afternoon?'

'Nothing much, you know.'

'Fantastic! Ready to play?'

'Yes, mate.'

'All right – now, you know the rules, Marvy?'

'No,' he says.

'I'm going to start the clock ticking. You say stop when you think you've won enough,

my impression
of a double
ended fish.

and it's yours to keep. But don't leave it too late. If the bomb explodes, you end up empty-handed!'

'Yeah, mate, no worries, mate.'

'Okay. Clock's ticking.'

Danny switches tapes and presses play.

tick tick tick tick tick tick tick

He picks up an empty Gladwrap tube and puts one end to the telephone and the other to his mouth.

'Twenty dollars,' he says. The tube gives his voice the spacey echo of the real voice. It's this sort of attention to detail that makes our practical jokes so special.

tick tick tick tick tick tick tick

Marvin says nothing.

'One hundred and sixty-three dollars,' says Danny, obviously enjoying himself.

'Three hundred and fifteen dollars.'

Silence. This guy's got nerves of steel. Either that or he's really greedy. Most people would have bailed out by now.

'Three hundred and eighty-three dollars.'

Danny looks at me. I shrug.

'Four hundred and forty-four dollars!'

A hammerhead shark

says Danny.

tick tick tick tick tick tick tick

'Five hundred dollars.'

'Stop!' says Marvin.

I signal to Danny to stop the tape.

'Marvin?'

'Yes?'

'Do you know what you've just done?'

'No, mate, did I do something wrong?'

'Wrong? Marvin, you have just won five hundred dollars! What do you think about that?'

'Oh, mate! That's fantastic! I can't believe it! Mum – I just won five hundred dollars!'

Marvin's mother starts squealing in the background. She's so loud, I have to hold the receiver away from my ear. Danny can hear it too. He's rolling around on the floor killing himself laughing.

'Hey, Marvy,' I say. 'What are you going to do with all that money?'

'I don't know,' says Marvin. 'I don't know. I've never won anything like this!'

'Well congratulations, Marvy. Now, if you can stay on the line while we get some

Are you UGLY. Now Dr. Griffith's Corrective Surgery can end your embarrassment.

TRY THIS,

↓

OR THIS, ↓

OR THIS. ↓

88

A parrot fish.

details, Elton John is going to take us back and show us how to do the Crocodile Rock. This is Triple B FM where – like Marvin Bonwick – we make your dreams come true. Good on ya, Marvy!'

'Thanks, mate!' he says.

Danny starts playing 'Crocodile Rock'.

We're about to yell, 'Just kidding, you stupid idiot!' when I hear a strange sound on the other end of the line. Like somebody crying.

I can hear Marvin talking.

'It's okay, Mum, it's okay. You should be happy!'

'I am happy,' she says.

Why would she be crying?

Danny's laughing so hard I'm worried he's going to wet himself.

'Shhh!' I tell him. 'Shut up!'

'What's wrong?' he says.

'I'm not sure,' I tell him. 'Just keep the noise down.'

Danny screws up his face.

'Marvy, are you still there?' I say.

'Yeah, mate, sorry, Mum's a bit emotional.'

ARE YOU TROUBLED BY ACNE (ZITS)

Yes.

Try Dr Griffith's Miracle Cure.

BURN THEM OFF WITH THIS MINI ACNE STRIPPER (It really works)

89
kc

A flathead.

KICK ME

'That's understandable,' I say. 'Five hundred dollars is a lot of money.'

'Yeah,' says Marvin. 'Especially for us . . . see . . . since Dad died we've been really struggling. Mum has to work pretty long hours to hold things together. This money is really going to help out. You've no idea how much it means to us.'

As Marvin talks I feel smaller and smaller. How was I to know his dad died? He didn't say anything. Not that he would have told me – I don't know him that well. But someone could have said something.

'Yeah, ah, um, glad to be able to help out, Marvy. Now if I could just get your address . . .'

Well, what else can I say? Somehow, 'Just kidding, you stupid idiot' doesn't seem quite as witty as it did a few minutes ago.

Danny's stopped laughing. He's frowning and looking at me like I'm off my nut.

'What?' he says.

I wave him away with my hand.

I take down Marvy's address.

'Thanks, Marvy. We'll send you a letter in the next few days with details of how to

Then, try eating his indoor plants to stumps. He'll be very impressed

I'm still bored

collect your payment.'

'Chris,' says Marvy, 'can I just say that you've made me and my mum really happy today – thanks a lot.'

'Don't mention it,' I say, and hang up.

'Are you out of your mind?' says Danny.

'His dad died.'

'So?'

'They really need the money.'

'So you promised it to them?'

I nod.

'Oh, man . . .' Danny is shaking his head.

'His mum was crying, Dan. He said they've been really struggling. I couldn't tell them it was just a joke. I couldn't.'

'So, you're going to send him five hundred dollars because you feel bad about a little practical joke?'

'It's not a *little* practical joke,' I say. 'It is an almighty stuff-up.'

'Know what I reckon?' says Danny.

'What?'

'Just do nothing. That way there's no need to explain. There's nothing to trace it back to us.'

HEALTH WARNING.

Dr Griffith's MIRACLE ACNE CURE, as advertized on Pg 89 of this book, should carry the following warning.

"Under some circumstances this cure may cause all of the skin on your face to char and fall off in great lumps. If these symptoms persist, see your local undertaker."

Otherwise it's ok!

Don't turn this next page or I'll explode.

91

KICK ME

'But what if they ring the radio station?'

'The radio station won't know anything about it,' says Danny. 'Marvin will realise it was a joke.'

'But that's terrible!' I say. 'Think how he'll feel. That's even worse than admitting it was a hoax. After all they've been through! No – we've got to get them that money.'

'What do you propose? Rob a bank?'

'No – we'll wash cars, mow lawns, pool all our pocket-money – and then we'll invest it in a high-interest bank account. We'll have the money in no time.'

'We?' says Danny.

'What do you mean?'

'*You* made the call.'

'You helped me.'

'But it was your idea.'

'You didn't say no.'

Danny hits himself on the head with his open palm. 'Do you have any idea how many cars we'll have to wash to earn that much money?!'

The phone rings.

I pick it up.

'Hello.'

'Hi, could I speak to Andy Griffiths?'

'Speaking.'

'Hi, Andy. Chris Robbins from Triple B FM here.'

My stomach drops. He must have found out I've been impersonating him! Marvin Bonwick must have rung him back to check if the call was legit! When he found out it was a trick he would have guessed it was me.

'Who is it?' says Danny.

I put my hand over the receiver. 'It's Chris Robbins! He must know! What do I do?'

'Talk to him,' says Danny. 'He can't prove anything.'

'Andy?' says Chris. 'Are you still there?'

'Yes,' I say. 'I'm here.'

'Thought we'd lost you for a minute.'

'Just a bit surprised,' I say. 'What can I do for you?'

'Well,' says Chris, 'I've just pulled your name out of the barrel to play Beat the Bomb – but if you'd rather not . . .'

'Are you kidding?' I shout. 'Of course I want to!'

CUP DAY, the year 2000.

...And still Phar Lap brings up the year...

Don't turn the page ... or I'll turn into an electrical appliance.

KICK ME

It's like a dream. What are the odds of something like this happening? A million to one? Nah – more like a squillion to one.

'Well, stand by,' says Chris. 'We're about to go to air. I'll just play a couple of ads and a station ID and then you're on. Oh, and by the way, Andy?'

'Yes?'

'Turn your radio off. We will be transmitting on a ten-second delay and it can get a little confusing.'

Through the earpiece of the telephone I hear a jingle for Cheapies carpet-cleaning service. Talk about *déjà vu*. If Danny wasn't right next to me I'd swear it was him playing another prank.

Then the Triple B station ID starts. Comets and meteorites again. 'Triple B – taking you back to the sixties and seventies...'

Then Chris starts speaking.

'Good afternoon. Chris Robbins with you on Triple B, and to play Beat the Bomb this hour we have Andy Griffiths on the line. How are you doin', Andy?'

PARTS
of
The
BODY.
——
NO. 15

BIG TOE,
with trapdoor
to allow
toe bone
to get out
for a
smoko
every now
and
then.

'Pretty good.'

'Great! What are you up to this afternoon?'

I wonder what he would say if I told him I was impersonating him and making prank Beat the Bomb phone calls. But I decide against it. I need the cash.

'Nothing much, you know.'

'Fantastic! Ready to play Beat the Bomb?'

'I sure am.'

'All right – now, you know the rules, Andy?'

'Yes,' I say, but he explains them anyway.

'Okay. Clock's ticking,' says Chris.

'Twenty dollars,' says the voice from outer space.

tick tick tick tick tick tick tick

I'd be happy with twenty. Maybe I should stop it right now. Those bombs can go off pretty fast sometimes.

'Twenty-five dollars.'

tick tick tick tick tick tick tick

'One hundred and forty-eight dollars.'

I want to stop, but I can't. It's like I'm frozen. If I can just keep my nerve . . .

'Two hundred and ninety dollars.'

HEALTH TIP.
If your brain starts leaking out of your ear,

place an old cork in your ear hole and hammer it in.

Your toast's ready.

KICK ME

tick tick tick tick tick tick tick

'Four hundred and sixty-six dollars.'

The ticking is deafening. Any minute now the bomb is going to explode and I'll be splattered all over the room. But still I can't speak.

'Five hundred and two dollars.'

I can't stand it any more.

'Stop!' I yell.

'Andy?'

'Yes?'

'Do you know what you've just done?'

'Yes,' I say in a dream.

'You have just won five hundred and two dollars! What do you think about that?'

I can't speak.

Danny's jumping up and down.

'How much?' he's saying. 'How much?!'

'Five hundred and two,' I say.

Danny hoots.

'Hey, Andy,' says Chris. 'What are you going to do with all that money?'

A vision of a pile of Mars bars as high as Mount Kosciusko fills my head. It merges into a tower of CDs and a stereo system loud

An old piece of wood

(Ask yourself, "Where has it come from?" "Where was it when Kurt Cobain was found dead?")

Didn't I ask you *not* to turn the page?

enough to blow my ears off. And then it dissolves into a blinding vision of flashing lights and beeps and explosions as I imagine spending an entire weekend in Timezone. But then I think of Marvin. And his mum.

'I'm not sure,' I say. 'Maybe I'll give it to a friend.'

Danny raises his eyebrows.

'Well, good on ya, Andy,' says Chris. 'Now, if you can stay on the line while we confirm your details, we've got something special coming up. Do you like John Farnham, Andy?'

I can't stand him, but I'll say anything for five hundred and two bucks.

'*Like* him? I *love* him!' I lie.

'Well, this is for you mate,' he says over the start of 'You're the Voice'. 'This is Triple B FM where – like Andy Griffiths – we make your dreams, and your friends' dreams, come true. Good on ya, Andy!'

'Thanks, mate,' I say.

My head is spinning. I'm trying to work out if I'm the most fantastically lucky person or the biggest loser in the world. I mean,

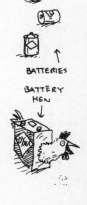

BATTERIES

BATTERY
HEN

Don't turn the page or I'll turn into a Septic Tank.

KICK
ME

having to pretend I like John Farnham is bad enough, but having one of his songs dedicated to me is much, much worse.

'Are you going to give that money to me?' says Danny. He's practically drooling all over the carpet.

'No,' I say. 'What makes you think that?'

'You said you were going to give it to a friend.'

'Yes, but not you,' I say.

'Then who?'

'Marvin.'

His jaw drops.

'You're kidding!'

So you think a cockroach has an I.Q. of 120, oh? That'd make me twice as smart as you. Try again.

'No,' I say.

'All of it?'

WOW!! I've been run over by a HONDA 750cc...

'No, not all of it. After I pay Marvin what we owe him there will be two dollars left over. We can go halves in that if you like.'

'Thanks, mate,' says Danny, staring at the carpet. 'You're a real pal.'

'Don't mention it,' I say. 'What are friends for?'

HA. HA. HA Tricked You!!

Born to Die

Well, I finally did it.

I've been thinking about it for ages and I kept putting it off, but this morning I finally did it.

I got a tattoo.

It's a skull with two eagle wings curving up over the top. The skull has these evil green eyes and a sort of long, thin red moustache that arcs upwards next to the wings. And running across the bottom of the skull is a small ribbon-shaped banner. And inside the banner are the words BORN TO DIE.

Didn't cost much either. Normally, it would have cost $2.95, but I got it on special at

Target for ninety-five cents.

And the best thing about it is that it didn't even hurt.

I just removed the protective sheet and pressed the sticky side firmly on to my skin. Then I wet the top of it with a sponge, waited for thirty seconds and peeled off the backing.

Yeah, so it's not real – but it's so realistic you'd never know the difference. And the amazing thing is, it makes me feel different. Bigger. Tougher. Bolder. Nobody's going to want to kick sand in my face and steal my girlfriend when they see I've got such a wicked-looking tat. Not that I have a girlfriend right at the moment, but as soon as they see my tattoo I bet every girl in school will want to go out with me – even the teachers.

The packet says it will last for days – almost forever. It also says I'll be able to shock my friends and family. But it's not my friends and family I'm interested in shocking. It's my enemies: Steve Lik and Robert Leech.

Steve Lik lives at the bottom of the hill. He's a few years older than me, but we used to muck around a bit together on the

weekends. Until he started hanging around with Robert Leech.

Robert Leech is a wiry-haired geek who lives over on the other side of the hill.

He's got a face like a rat, with a really thin pointy nose and beady brown eyes. He thinks he's really good because he rides a fifteen-speed racer and smokes rollies. He doesn't like me much. Well, to be truthful, he hates my guts. I don't know what I did to make him hate me so much. Being born, I suppose. Robert Leech is just that sort of guy.

Lately, him and Lik have taken to waiting for me at the bottom of the hill outside Lik's place and they won't let me pass until I tell them the password. Today is no exception. I turn the corner into my street and they're both there, like they've been waiting for me. Leech is sitting in the middle of the footpath. He's got his jaws rigid and his lips tight as he blows a series of smoke rings. Lik is leaning against his letterbox with a yellow bucket in his hand. I could try crossing the road, but I know they'd just come after me. I pretend to ignore them.

'Well, well, well,' says Leech, in between smoke rings. 'If it isn't our old mate Andy.'

Lik smirks.

'Do you mind if I just go past?' I say, moving to step around him. But Leech's hand shoots out and grabs my ankle.

'Not so fast,' he says. 'Say please.'

'Please,' I say, looking straight ahead.

'Say "pretty please",' he says. '"With sugar on top".'

'Pretty please with sugar on top,' I say.

'Say "pretty please with sugar on top, Sir!"'

I know from experience that this can go on for a long time. But today I don't have to put up with this crap, because I've got a tattoo. I casually roll up the sleeves of my windcheater. The tattoo is still there on my right forearm. The skull's eyes seem to be flashing.

'Look, I don't want any trouble,' I say. 'Just let me past . . . or else.'

Leech laughs. 'Or else what?' He is too busy blowing smoke rings to notice my tattoo. But I can see that Lik has seen it. He's already backing off.

'Come on, Leechy. That'll do.'

AMAZING EYE TRICK #2 ANSWER

Have you forgotten? You promised your mum you'd take the washing off the line. And it's been raining!! You're in trouble.

102
You could warn me.

Leech stops laughing. 'Huh?'

Lik steps across to him and whispers in his ear.

Leech jumps up from the footpath, his eyes fixed on my forearm. He takes a couple of steps backwards.

'Can I pass now?' I ask.

'Yeah, of c-course,' says Leech. 'We were just kidding around. Just a bit of fun, you know.'

'Fun? That's what you call fun?'

Leech and Lik are standing there frozen, like a couple of stunned rabbits. I'm not sure whether they're scared of the tattoo or just the way it makes me act, but I don't really care. I flex the muscles in my forearm – which is a hard thing to do really, because I don't have that many. But my skull doesn't mind. It ripples and seems to grin in response, like it's enjoying it. I guess I should be scared, but I feel strangely calm. Like I can do whatever the heck I want. Why not pull out all the stops and teach them a lesson they'll never forget?

Lik is still holding the yellow bucket.

'What's in the bucket?' I say.

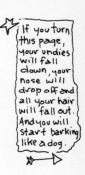If you turn this page, your undies will fall down, your nose will drop off and all your hair will fall out. And you will start barking like a dog.

You know perfectly well there's a hook there.

'Slugs,' says Lik.

'How come?' I ask, knowing full well that they get their jollies out of inventing new and horrible ways for slugs to die.

'Um, er, well, my dad asked me to. They've been eating his rose bushes.'

'Don't give me that,' I say. 'Let 'em go.'

Lik looks at Leech. Leech nods. Lik tips the bucket, and about twenty fat grey slugs fall into the shrubbery.

I watch them helplessly trying to untangle themselves from one another and shake my head.

'You know,' I say, 'maybe it's just me, but I don't find that very funny.'

Lik and Leech are both silent.

'And another thing I don't find very funny is you two hassling me every time I walk past. It's got to stop.'

'Sorry,' says Lik. 'We were just mucking around. How about a milkshake to make up for it?'

I should leave it here and just keep walking up the hill, but I'm enjoying my new-found power to much. I remember the cool milkshakes that Lik used to make for me back in the days when we were friends. Two heaped teaspoons of malt, eggs, ice cream and about half a bottle of chocolate syrup. Hardly any room for the milk. Beautiful.

'Thought you'd never ask,' I say.

'Okay,' says Lik. 'I'll go get you one, won't be a sec.'

'No, not a takeaway,' I say. 'I think I'll drink it inside, if that's okay with you. Sun's kind of hot today.'

skeleton staff
↓

Leech and Lik look at each other.

'Yeah, Andy,' says Lik. 'Of course. Come in.'

We start walking up the drive. I'm so cool I can't believe it.

Inside, I pick the best seat in the loungeroom and plonk my feet up on the coffee table. There's a pile of magazines on top of the table, so I push them all off on to the carpet with my feet.

'I think I'll just wait here while you make my milkshake,' I say.

'Sure, fine,' says Lik.

I grab the remote and turn on the television. I turn up the sound full-blast so that it's distorting.

Lik pokes his head around the door.

'Hey, Andy!' he says.

'What?'

'Can you turn that down a bit?'

'No,' I say. 'I like it loud.'

Lik just stands there like he's not sure whether to rip the remote out of my hand and shove it down my throat or just leave it.

'Wanna make something of it?' I say.

'No,' he says, 'of course not. You're the guest. What flavour milkshake do you want?'

'Chocolate, of course,' I say.

'Coming up,' he says and goes back into the kitchen.

Good night frank. See you same time next week.

I start flicking through the channels on the remote. 'Playschool' on Channel Two. The presenters are pretending to be kookaburras. They're singing a song.

'Kookaburra sits on the old gum tree, merry merry king of the bush is he . . .'

I know exactly how that kookaburra feels. I'm the king and Lik and Leech are my subjects. They will do anything I tell them to. I watch a bit more of 'Playschool', then turn it off.

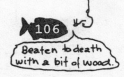

106 Beaten to death with a bit of wood.

'What's taking so long?' I call.

'Almost ready,' yells Leech.

I hear the high-pitched whine of the blender. My mouth starts watering. Steve Lik's milkshakes are really something else.

The blender stops.

'I don't want it in the container, either,' I say. 'I want it in a glass. With a straw!'

'No worries,' calls Lik.

SIMPSON and his Echidna.

Leech enters the room with the milkshake on a tray. Lik is right behind him.

Leech places the tray on top of the coffee table. The milkshake is in one of those old-fashioned glasses with ridges down the side and a crazy straw sticking out. There is a scoop of chocolate ice-cream sitting on top.

A really tough bloke

Lik picks up the glass and gives it to me. Then they both kneel down on either side of my chair and stare at me.

'Do you mind?' I say.

'No,' says Leech, his lips curling into a slight smile.

'Well, what are you waiting for?'

'We just want to watch you drink it,' says Lik.

107

Scaled, filleted, cooked and eaten.

'We just want to watch you enjoy it,' says Leech.

There's something about the way he says 'enjoy' that I don't like.

Tough Blokes eat petals...

Bicycle Pedals!

I push my arm forward to make sure they remember who's boss here. I look at them, look at my tattoo and look back at them to make sure they've got the message.

But they just start laughing. My stomach drops.

'Would you mind sharing the joke with me?' I say.

'Should we?' says Lik.

'Yes,' says Leech. 'I think we should.'

Leech pulls up his sleeve. Lik pulls up his sleeve.

On each of their arms – in almost exactly the same place as mine – is a skull with green eyes and a long red moustache.

I look at them.

They look at me.

The room is very quiet.

'Well, drink up,' says Lik. 'We're waiting.'

'Um,' I say, 'look, thanks for the milkshake and everything, but I'm not really that thirsty. I

Then who'd tell you what page number it is.

might just get going.'

I sit forward to get up, but Lik pushes me back into my seat.

'After we've gone to all this trouble? Surely you've got a minute just to drink a milkshake. You can't waste it.'

'Okay,' I say. 'But then I've really got to get going.'

'Sure,' says Lik. 'Drink up.'

I guess there are worse punishments.

I put the glass up to my lips.

'Oh, there's just one thing,' says Leech. 'Hope you don't mind, but we couldn't find any chocolate syrup.'

I'm starting to sweat.

'That's okay,' I say, trying to keep cool. 'What did you use instead?'

'Slugs,' says Leech. 'Now drink up.'

WAITING FOR THE PRINCIPAL?

Charm him by swallowing all the school goldfish.

GULP!

invisipills

Mrs Wharton is stomping around the library. She's telling kids off for talking. She's telling kids off for leaning back on their chairs. She's practically telling kids off for breathing. You name it, and she's telling them off for it.

I reckon she's wasted as a librarian. Mrs Wharton should have been the governor of a high-security prison. That'd be one prison where they wouldn't have to worry about the prisoners talking, leaning back on their chairs or returning their library books late.

The only person Mrs Wharton has not told off so far this lesson is me. That's because I'm working so hard. It's pretty rare for me to work this hard, but I have a big assignment on Antarctic explorers due in on Monday. It's worth 50 per cent of our end of year mark and I've only just started it.

The trouble is, Danny is sitting at the desk next to mine and he keeps going on and on about how he wants to be invisible. He won't shut up. He's been talking about it for weeks now. Normally, I wouldn't mind, but I don't want to risk getting kicked out of the library because I need to use the Internet.

'Psst! Andy!' says Danny.

'Shhh!' I say to him. 'Do you want to get us kicked out?'

'No,' he says, 'just tell me what you reckon. If I got a can of spray-paint and painted myself pink and painted my whole room pink and everything in it pink – do you think I'd be invisible then?'

'Well, maybe,' I whisper. 'As long as you stayed in your room. But once you left, you'd be a bit conspicuous.'

'Oh,' he says.

He's quiet for a few seconds. Then he

AURHH SPIDER

leans over again.

'Psst!'

'What!?' I say. I'm getting really impatient.

'What does "conspicuous" mean?'

'It means you'd stand out like a pimple on a pumpkin! Now would you shut up and do some work – and stop interrupting me!'

'Yeah, sorry, mate,' he says. 'But honestly, do you reckon it would work?'

'For the last time, shut up!'

I reach into my pencil case for a lolly. Well, they're *supposed* to be lollies. They're really just those little multi-coloured balls with no taste. Nobody likes them, except three-year-olds – and that's only because they don't know any better. I'm only eating them because they were a present from my granny. It would have been rude to throw them away.

I crunch one between my teeth.

Danny leans over.

'What are those?' he says.

Suddenly I have an idea of how to get rid of him.

Mrs Wharton is up at the loans counter checking out some books. This gives me a few minutes.

'Danny, what would you say if I had a way of really making you invisible?'

'How?'

I pass him the tube of lollies.

'I was waiting until your birthday to give you these, but since you want to be invisible so badly, you might as well have them now.'

'What are they?' he says.

'They're invisipills. They make you invisible.'

'For real?'

'Absolutely.'

'Where'd you get them?' he says.

'I made them in science. I got the recipe off the Net.'

Danny hits his head with his hand. 'Oh, man! Why didn't I think of that! Which site?'

'I'd rather not say. The recipe was smuggled out of the Pentagon. Top-secret stuff. I could get into a lot of trouble if I'm caught.'

'Have you tried them?'

'Yep.'

'And?'

'They're pretty amazing. One pill will make you completely invisible for about half an hour.'

'Wow! How come you didn't tell me?'

'Like I said, I was keeping it for a surprise for your birthday.'

'Can I try one?'

'Sure. Just one, though. They're pretty powerful. And you've got to promise me one thing.'

'What?' says Danny.

'That after you've taken it you'll go outside and let me work.'

'No problem,' he says.

He takes a lolly from the tube.

His eyes are wide as he puts it on to his tongue, closes his mouth and swallows.

'Well?' he says. 'Am I invisible?'

'Not yet,' I say. 'It takes a few minutes.'

Danny's holding his hands out in front of him, fingers outstretched.

'Have I faded even a little bit?' he says. 'What do you reckon?'

I screw up my eyes, pretending to study him.

'Yes – definitely!' I say. 'No doubt about it.'

'Cool!' he says.

I glance up. Mrs Wharton has finished at the loans counter and is prowling the library again.

'You're fading fast now,' I say. 'I can hardly see you.'

'No I'm not,' he says. 'I can still see me as clear as anything.'

'Yeah – you're meant to, you dork. That's the way the pills are designed. You can see yourself, but nobody can see you. If you couldn't see yourself, you wouldn't know where you were and you'd get lost.'

'Oh, I get it,' he says. 'So, am I invisible yet?'

'Where are you?'

'I'm right here!'

'No you're not. Not as far as I can see. Your chair is empty.'

'Can you still hear me?'

'Yes. Now go outside! Remember our deal?'

'Okay,' says Danny. 'I'm outa here.'

Danny gets up out of his seat and walks off.

Mrs Wharton is coming slowly towards me.

I go back to my assignment and do my

Amazing EYE TRICK Nº5
Which of these two circles is the bigger?
a. ○
b. ◯
(Look carefully.)
ANS: Pg 129

Dr. Griffith's Corrective Surgery

BEFORE

AFTER.

I am!

best imitation of a serious student.

Just as she's walking past my desk I hear the most enormous belch.

It's so loud it practically rocks the foundations of the library.

For a moment I think it was Mrs Wharton. But that – of course – is ridiculous. Only Danny can do them that loud.

I look around. Sure enough, Danny is killing himself laughing in the aisle.

Mrs Wharton stops.

'Excuse me!' she says. 'Was that you?'

'No, Mrs Wharton,' I say.

'Then who was it, pray tell? A ghost?'

'I don't know, Mrs Wharton. But it wasn't me.'

'I don't believe you. What are those?' she says, pointing at the lollies, which Danny has thoughtfully left sitting on my desk in full view.

'Um . . . lollies, Mrs Wharton.'

'I presume you know the rule about eating in the library.'

'Yes, Mrs Wharton.'

'And you know that it specifically excludes

chewing gum, bubble gum *and* lollies?'

'Yes, Mrs Wharton. I'll get rid of them.'

'No you won't,' she says, '*I* will.'

She holds out her hand. I pick up the tube and give it to her. Little does she realise she's doing me a big favour.

She walks on up the aisle without another word.

That was close. I'm going to kill Danny after school. With any luck, he's kept his promise and is outside by now.

Thump!

A book lands on the carpet next to my desk. It's *The Wonderful World of Freshwater Fish*, and I have no doubt who threw it.

Another book sails over the top of the shelves and lands on my desk. Whack! Another hits the top edge of the desk and bounces off on to the student in front of me.

'Ouch!' he yells, turning to me. 'Quit it!'

I shrug.

'It wasn't me,' I say.

The books keep coming. And so does Mrs Wharton.

'Stand up!' she says. 'Would you mind

Great
Places
to Hide.

telling me what's going on here?'

'Somebody is throwing books over the tops of the shelves,' I say.

'Who?'

'I don't know.'

She strides off and checks each of the aisles. Any moment now she's going to see Danny and chuck him out. Good riddance I reckon.

'I can't see anybody,' she says. 'Perhaps you'd better tell me how these books really ended up on the floor.'

I don't know what to say.

Over Mrs Wharton's shoulder I can see the A–G fiction shelf rocking back and forth. Danny's gone crazy. The excitement of thinking he's invisible has gone to his head. I've got to stop him before he goes too far.

'Excuse me, Mrs Wharton,' I say. 'Back in a minute.'

'Where do you think you're going?'

I dash to the seriously rocking shelf to try to pull Danny away and bring him to his senses, but it's already too late. The shelf tilts too far to the right. All the books fall

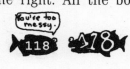

on to the carpet. The force of the bookshelf striking the next shelf pushes it over and the combined weight of these two pushes the third shelf over. Just like a row of dominoes. Except heavier. And louder.

There is silence. Nobody can believe what they've just seen.

I turn around. Mrs Wharton is speechless. She is opening and closing her mouth like a fish.

But Danny hasn't finished yet.

He's approaching Mrs Wharton from behind, one of her prized hanging-basket ferns in his hand. The ferns that she waters so lovingly every morning before school. The ferns that if anyone so much as looks at them – let alone touches them – they cop one of Mrs Wharton's famous glares.

Danny's staring straight ahead and carrying the pot plant in his raised outstretched arms, like it's the Australian Football League Premiership Cup.

'No!' I yell, but it's like he's possessed.

He tips it upside down over Mrs Wharton's head. Fern fronds and clumps of dirt and little white fertiliser pellets spill all over her hair, down her face and on to her yellow dress. They collect in a pile at her feet.

Danny is just standing there laughing. Poor guy. He still thinks he's invisible.

Mrs Wharton wheels around.

'Just what do you think you're doing?' she says to him.

'Who?' he says.

'You!' she says, going red in the face.

'But you can't see me,' says Danny. 'I'm invisible!'

'Invisible? Well, we'll see about that!' she says.

WEIRD PLACES TO HIDE.

HUMAN BODY PARTS No 47B.

The Tongue

She reaches out, grabs his ear and twists it at least 360 degrees – and then – judging by the expression on Danny's face – another 360 degrees after that.

Danny drops to his knees in pain.

'Oww! Oww! Let go!' he says.

'There,' she says. 'Feeling a little more visible now?'

I must admit I'm rather enjoying the spectacle. After all, Danny had no qualms about getting me into trouble.

Now you're being silly!

120

Mrs Wharton lets go of his ear.

'Now,' she says, looking from Danny to me, 'both of you pack up your books, and get straight to the principal's office! And consider yourselves banned from the library for the rest of the year.'

Both of us? The rest of the year? Great. There goes my history assignment. And my English wide reading. And my social studies research. How could Danny be so dumb?

I gather up my books. There's no use arguing.

Mrs Wharton escorts us to the door and slams it behind us.

'Danny,' I say, turning to face him, 'you are a prize drongo. Did you really think . . .'

But I don't finish my question. Danny's not there.

'Dan? Where are you?'

I hear a giggle and then a tremendous belch in my right ear. It's so loud it almost ruptures my ear-drum.

I spin around.

'Danny?'

But there's no sign of him – no visible sign

anyway – just the sound of his crazy laughter echoing down the empty corridor.

The principal can wait. I'm going straight to sick bay.

I'm feeling a little faint myself.

A TerrIBLE christmas and a CRappy new year

Sunday afternoon.

Jen's Christmas cards are sitting on the table. All fifty thousand of them in three big stacks. The envelopes aren't sealed, so I figure that means she wants me to open them and have a look.

I open the top envelope. The card has a picture of a big jolly Santa's face on it.

The message on the inside reads: Dear Kerrie, wishing you a Merry Christmas and a Happy New Year, love Jen.

Very original . . . not!

The second card has exactly the same picture on it.

And inside Jen has written exactly the same greeting: Dear Sandra, wishing you a Merry Christmas and a Happy New Year, love Jen.

She has written the same thing on every card. The only bit that changes is the name of the person she's sending it to.

There's only one thing to do.

I grab some Tippex, a black marker and set to work.

SANTA BOARS!

I don't have much time. Jen will be wanting to catch the six o'clock post.

On the first card I draw heavy dark eyebrows over Santa's twinkling eyes. He's not looking quite so jolly now.

But still, it's not enough. I draw a scar running from the corner of his right eye to the corner of his mouth. I black out one of his front teeth and give him a black eye. And just for fun I add a couple of Frankenstein bolts to each side of his neck. That's better. Completely psycho.

Now for the greeting on the inside. Merry Christmas? I don't think so. I change the M on *Merry* to a T, cross out the Y and add

IBLE to the end. And a happy new year? Not if I replace the H on *Happy* with CR. Much nicer . . . A TerrIBLE Christmas and a CRappy New Year.

I go through the rest of the cards, changing the greetings and adding eyebrows, scars, moustaches, nose-rings, eyebrow-rings, tattoos, antennae and Martian ears to the Santas. By the time I'm finished, no two Santas are alike. The only thing they have in common is that if you saw any of them coming towards you on the street, you'd turn and run the other way.

NEW SITE FOR THE BEST PRACTICAL JOKE EVER. Pg 70

I put each card carefully back into its envelope so it doesn't look like they've been messed with.

And — as if brightening up her Christmas cards isn't enough — I even take the trouble to find Jen and ask her if she'd like me to run them down to the postbox for her.

SLEEP PILLS

FOR Santa

She asks me if I'm feeling all right.

I tell her that Christmas is a time for giving and that doing things for her makes me happy.

What..?

She accuses me of sucking up because it's Christmas.

If only she knew . . .

The postbox is over the other side of the hill.

There are so many cards I almost get repetitive strain injury putting them in the box. But at last they're all posted.

I'm feeling pretty happy with myself.

Jen's friends all think they're *so* sophisticated. I can just imagine the looks on their faces when they see their mutant Santas. They'll think Jen has lost her mind. Maybe they'll kick her out of the gang for being so childish. That would be excellent. Then maybe she could get some new friends. Some nice ones.

And then an awful thought occurs to me.

What if Jen's friends retaliate? What if they start sending cards back to her wishing *her* a terrible Christmas — or worse? I wouldn't put it past them.

It's not going to take Jen long to figure

out that I had something to do with it.

And then she'll punish me by giving me a horrible present – or even worse – no present at all.

Maybe this joke wasn't such a great idea . . .

I have to get those cards back out of the box!

Luckily, the postbox has a parcel handle. Being Christmas time, the box will probably be so full that Jen's cards will be right on top. Getting them back is going to be easy.

I pull the handle towards me and slide my arm into the parcel slot. Standing on the tips of my toes, I ease the handle away from me and try to curl my arm down into the box. But it doesn't work. My arm is jammed against the back of the parcel chute. My fingers are nowhere near the letters. There must be a better way.

I could get a fishing line with a hook on the end of it and try fishing them out. No, that would take too long.

It's getting late. I'm getting desperate.

Perhaps I could build a fire around the

bottom of the box so that it heats up and becomes like a huge oven and incinerates everything inside it.

Or maybe I could grab the hose from the house opposite and fill the box with water. Then the ink on the front of the envelopes would smudge and run and the post office won't know where to send them.

They are both brilliant plans, but neither would be fair to the innocent letters already in the box. I don't want to stop them getting through – I just want Jen's letters back.

I hear a squeal of brakes behind me.

I turn around. It's the postman!

'Am I glad to see you,' I say. 'I just posted some letters, but I think I forgot to put the postcodes on and I was wondering if you could get them back for me.'

'Sorry, mate,' says the postman, 'I can't help ya. I'm not allowed to do that.'

He puts a sack underneath the door and turns the key.

Hundreds of letters flow into the sack.

'Besides, it'd take ages to find your letters in amongst this lot,' he says. 'Go down to the

DO YOU
HAVE
TO VISIT
THE
SCHOOL
PRINCIPAL?

Charm
him/her
by sticking
bananas
up your
nostrils.
Works
every
time.
TRUST
US!

post office. They might be able to help.'

'But I can't get there now,' I say. 'It's too late.'

He shrugs. 'Too bad.'

'Please?' I say. 'It's a matter of life and death.'

'So's my job,' says the postman. He gets into his van and zooms off.

So much for Christmas spirit.

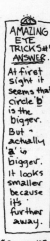

AMAZING EYE TRICKS#5 ANSWER.

At first sight it seems that circle 'b' is the bigger. But actually 'a' is bigger. It looks smaller because it's further away.

* see pg 137.

I don't see much of Jen for the rest of the week, until Friday afternoon. The mail arrives late. There's the usual boring letters for Mum and Dad, a couple of cards for Jen and, as usual, nothing for me.

I go to Jen's room and knock on her door.

'Yes?' she says.

'Some letters for you,' I say.

She opens the door. Her eyes are puffy, as if she's been crying. I hand her the envelopes. She takes them without a word and closes the door.

A few minutes later I hear loud sobs

What to wear for work experience!

The Accountants.

oh... oh !!

coming from her room.

I can guess why. It's just as I feared. Her friends are sending her horrible cards. I should confess, but how can I?

And what if Father Christmas finds out? He only comes to *good* boys and girls. What a dumb prank to play right before Christmas.

'Due to lack of space, the best practical joke ever has been moved to Pg 24.

It's the night before Christmas. I'm in the loungeroom. It's dark, except for the blinking of the Christmas tree lights.

I've just put out a glass of milk and some chocolate-chip cookies for Santa, like I do every year. I've laid a pillowslip on a chair and written my name on it in black marker so he'll know it's mine. I'm just adding a few last-minute items to my letter to Santa when I hear the unmistakable sounds of jingling and reindeer hooves on the roof.

He's early!

I quickly fold the letter and stuff it into the envelope.

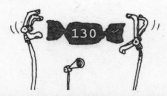

But before I can get out of the room, there is a huge crash. And then a stream of angry cursing. Well, I think it's cursing. Some of the words are new to me, but they sound like the sort of thing I'd get into trouble for repeating.

What to wear for work experience: At the Dentists

A cloud of black soot explodes from the fireplace, followed by Santa.

At least, I *think* it's Santa . . .

There's no big white beard or red suit, and he's as skinny as a rake. He is clad in black leather with chains and silver studs. His face is covered in a dark three-day-old growth and one of his front teeth is missing. He has a black eye and a scar running from the corner of his mouth to his ear. And worst of all, little Frankenstein bolts coming out of his neck.

HOURS OF FUN:

Saw all your family's Xmas presents in half.

He seems strangely familiar. Where have I seen this man before?

And then I remember.

I created him. He's one of the mutant Santas from Jen's Christmas cards.

'Stop right there, you little weasel!' he booms. 'It's time all *good* children were in

bed! What are you doing still up?'

'I-I-I was in bed,' I say, 'but then I remembered I'd forgotten to put out some cookies and a glass of milk for you.'

'Milk?' he snarls, and then spits into the fireplace. He picks up the glass and throws the milk in my face. 'Milk? What sort of a wuss do you think I am! Got anything stronger?'

'There's maybe a Coke in the fridge,' I say, wiping the milk from my eyes.

'I mean even stronger! It's cold out there dammit! And as for these . . .'

Santa picks up the chocolate-chip cookies in his bony hands and crumbles them into dust.

'These are for kids! I travel all the way from the North Pole and you think a few cookies will satisfy my hunger. I want a steak! Medium rare! Now!'

'I'll see what I can do,' I say. I run to the kitchen and open the freezer. There are no steaks. All we've got is veggie-burgers. Completely frozen. I guess they'll have to do. I grab the box and go back to the loungeroom.

Aughh... this is the end

Merry Christmas

Santa is scratching his bum.

'Well?' he says.

'How about a veggie-burger?' I say, offering the box.

He shakes his head.

'You're an idiot!' he says. 'I don't know why I waste my time. What's that in your other hand?'

I'm still holding my letter to Santa.

'It's a letter for you . . .' I say. 'With a few of the things I was hoping for . . .'

'Give it here!' he says, striding over and snatching it out of my hand.

But he doesn't read it. He wipes his nose with it, crumples it into a ball and throws it into the fireplace.

'I feel 100kg lighter and 10 years younger'

He sniffs loudly and reaches into a black duffle bag that's slung over his shoulder.

'Okay, Mr Vege-bleeding-tarian! Since you like vegetables so much, this is for you. Catch!'

He throws me a small silver ball.

It stinks.

'Open it,' he says.

I peel off a bit of the foil. The smell gets worse.

POP

133

'Keep going!'

I keep peeling the foil. It's a potato. Dark-grey. Mouldy. Stinking.

'Now,' says Santa, 'eat it!'

And he laughs and he laughs and that's when I wake up – with a horrible taste in my mouth – wishing I'd never played that stupid childish practical joke on Jen.

Christmas is now only five days away. I've had the rotten potato dream the last three nights in a row. I'm too scared to sleep. I've got to tell Jen what I've done.

I can hear her talking in the kitchen. I get out of bed. I've got to confess.

I open the kitchen door. Jen is yelling. She sees me and slams the telephone down.

'What do you want, you little snoop!' she snaps. She's holding a card. There's a ripped envelope on the floor.

'Nothing,' I say and go straight out. She's had another fight with another one of her friends. She'll probably be friendless

for the rest of her life.

And it's all my fault.

It's the night before Christmas. There's a large box wrapped in gold paper underneath the Christmas tree. I hadn't noticed it until now. My name's on the card. And it's from Jen! I hold it up to my ear and shake it. No clues. I peel a bit of the sticky tape away from one end of the paper to try to get a glimpse of what it is.

'Oh, hi,' says Jen. 'I see you've found your present.'

Sprung bad. I drop the present and turn around.

'Yes, I mean, no, I wasn't doing anything,' I stutter.

'It's okay,' she says. 'It's your present. Merry Christmas.'

'Thanks, Jen.'

But instead of making me happy it makes me feel even more guilty.

I betrayed her trust.

I defaced her cards.

All her friends hate her – and it's all my fault.

It's now or never.

'Um – Jen – this is probably a really cool present and all, but I really don't deserve it . . . you see, I've changed your cards . . . and I've been feeling really bad about it . . .'

'So it *was* you!' she says. 'I thought so!'

'I know it was dumb,' I say. 'But . . .'

'Dumb? No way! It was brilliant!'

'Huh?' I say, so surprised I almost fall over. 'But over the last couple of weeks you've seemed really upset – I thought it was my fault.'

'Oh that,' she laughs. 'I broke up with Rob, but it's no big deal. We made up last night.'

'So, you actually liked the cards?'

'My friends loved them!' she says. 'You've started a real craze. Come and see!'

She takes me to her bedroom.

This is a very special privilege. She once told me that if I ever came in here she would personally pull out each and every one of my teeth with a rusty pair of pliers –

CORPORATE
SANTA

without anaesthetic.

She points to an enormous bunch of cards on her window sill.

I can't believe my eyes.

On each of the cards there is a different sort of Santa. A sneering punk Santa with a safety pin through his nose. A long-haired heavy metal Santa playing a guitar solo on his reindeer's antlers. There're grunge Santas, hip-hop Santas, hippy Santas, Frankenstein Santas — even a dreadlocked Reggae Santa smoking a huge white cigar. Wow! Who would've ever thought Jen's friends had a sense of humour?

'Just promise me one thing,' says Jen. 'Don't tell anybody you changed the cards. See, they all think it was my idea and I'd kind of like to keep it that way.'

'Okay,' I say, 'as long as you promise me something.'

'What's that?'

'Don't breathe a word about this to Santa.'

Jen puts a finger up to her mouth. 'My lips are sealed,' she says.

SANTASTEIN'S MONSTER.

137

I was a Xmas Bon-Bon and I didn't even get a PARTY HAT... or a whistle !! That's it !! I've had enough !!! THIS IS THE END !!!

END

Website Discount Offer

Get 3 for 2 on any of the Help! series at www.panmacmillan.com

£1 postage and packaging costs to UK addresses, £2 for overseas

To buy the books with this special discount:

1. visit our website, www.panmacmillan.com
2. search by author or book title
3. add to your shopping basket

Closing date is 30 June 2011.

Full terms and conditions can be found at www.panmacmillan.com

Registration is required to purchase books from the website.

The offer is subject to availability of stock and applies to paperback editions only.

≋ panmacmillan.com